A Candlelight Ecstasy Romance®

"WHY DON'T YOU BELIEVE IN 'HAPPILY EVER AFTER'?" CAMERON SAT STARING OUT INTO THE RAINY AFTERNOON.

Lexy shrugged. "Because I think there are some people who were meant to settle down and some who weren't. As time has gone on I've come to believe that I am one of those for whom there will be no 'happily ever after.' Perhaps men find it hard to accept in their lives women who expect to be equals."

"Do you think I don't look on you as an equal?"

"You confuse it," she replied simply. "Intellectually you think of me as an equal. Emotionally you want to protect me, take care of me—possess me."

"I want to love you," Cameron replied, his voice full of sorrow.

CANDLELIGHT ECSTASY ROMANCES®

330   A GLIMPSE OF PARADISE, *Cathie Linz*
331   WITH EACH CARESS, *Anne Silverlock*
332   JUST A KISS AWAY, *JoAnna Brandon*
333   WHEN MIDNIGHT COMES, *Edith Delatush*
334   MORE THAN A DREAM, *Lynn Patrick*
335   HOLD CLOSE THE MEMORY, *Heather Graham*
336   A VISION OF LOVE, *Melanie Catley*
337   DIAMOND IN THE ROUGH, *Joan Grove*
338   LOVING LESSONS, *Barbara Andrews*
339   ROMANTIC ROULETTE, *Jackie Black*
340   HIDEAWAY, *Carol Norris*
341   NO RESERVATIONS, *Molly Katz*
342   WANTED: MAN TO LOVE, *Evelyn Coate*
343   SURPRISE PACKAGE, *Emily Elliott*
344   TILL MORNING'S LIGHT, *Sheila Paulos*
345   A WHOLE LOT OF WOMAN, *Anna Hudson*
346   A TASTE OF HEAVEN, *Samantha Hughes*
347   HOPELESSLY DEVOTED, *Alexis Hill Jordan*
348   STEAL A RAINBOW, *Sue Gross*
349   SCARLET MEMORIES, *Betty Henrichs*
350   SPITFIRE, *Lori Copeland*
351   SO DEAR TO MY HEART, *Dorothy Ann Bernard*
352   IN DEFENSE OF PASSION, *Kit Daley*
353   NIGHTSONG, *Karen Whittenburg*

WALKING ON AIR

Michele Robbe

A CANDLELIGHT ECSTASY ROMANCE®

Published by
Dell Publishing Co., Inc.
1 Dag Hammarskjold Plaza
New York, New York 10017

ISBN: 0-440-19349-4

Printed in the United States of America

First printing—August 1985

This book is dedicated to:

Marcella, my mom:
> who never gives up on me;

April,
> who believes I can do things;

Kathy,
> who makes sure I do things
> (and types them);

Norma,
> who gives me moral support;
> and

M.L.S.,
> out of sheer perversity.

To Our Readers:

We have been delighted with your enthusiastic response to Candlelight Ecstasy Romances®, and we thank you for the interest you have shown in this exciting series.

In the upcoming months we will continue to present the distinctive sensuous love stories you have come to expect only from Ecstasy. We look forward to bringing you many more books from your favorite authors, and also the very finest work from new authors of contemporary romantic fiction.

As always, we are striving to present the unique, absorbing love stories that you enjoy most—books that are more than ordinary romance. Your suggestions and comments are always welcome. Please write to us at the address below.

Sincerely,

The Editors
Candlelight Romances
1 Dag Hammarskjold Plaza
New York, New York 10017

CHAPTER ONE

Alexandra Prince, known to friends and colleagues simply as Lexy, scuffed through the ankle-high grass, watching the long blades tangle around her black work boots. With her hands jammed in her pockets she ambled toward the runway a quarter mile away.

Behind her, walking in twos and threes, talking amiably among themselves, came the rest of the ground crew of the Vulcan Tire & Rubber Company airship, the *Andromeda*. Like Lexy, they all wore white shirts with blue and gold lettering and dark blue uniform pants. This was the last landing of the day, and everyone seemed to walk with a little more lightness to their step, realizing that soon they would be piling back on the crew bus to return to the Modoc Motel.

The fifteen ground crewmen assembled into formation—the gondola party in the middle with the crew chief holding the bright orange wind sock, and the linemen twenty yards farther out in front of them in two lines—to await the return of the blimp that was moving slowly across the brilliant blue Oregon sky. The June afternoon gave the airport and the airliners sitting on the taxiways the look of a mirage. Shimmering in the heat almost two miles away were the buildings and terminals of Portland International Airport.

All airports look alike, Lexy decided. Only the landscape around them changes. She drank in the awesome beauty of Mount Rainier, miles to the west, poking its white crown through a low cloud cover on the horizon. As she did daily, she thanked God for this wonderful job, which allowed her to leave Los Angeles for nearly six months out of the year.

The silver oval of the airship turned toward them, still more than a mile away. The black lettering VUL-CAN on the sides and the red fins stood out in the sunlight. It nosed into the wind, squaring up for a landing.

Lexy stood with two of the other crewmen, K. C. Gill, young and fuzzy-headed, and Kerry Larson, the tall, wiry heavy-duty mechanic for the operation. The two men chatted amiably about women, a subject Lexy had learned long ago to shut out. Instead she concentrated on the beauty of the day and the evening ahead, when she would be alone there, standing watch over the airship.

"Earth to Lexy, earth to Lexy," Kerry said.

She looked up at him, squinting into the sun behind her sunglasses. "I'm sorry, Kerry. What were you saying?"

Kerry grinned. "I asked what you thought of Cameron coming back."

Lexy shrugged. "I've never met the man. He left for the European operation right before I became a crewman."

"He's great," Kerry said. "You'll like him."

Something about the smirk that went with Kerry's statement irritated her.

"Sure I will. I've heard you guys talking about his exploits. You know what I think of womanizers like him." Lexy shook her head. "No, thanks."

K.C. sneered. "You're such a Puritan, Lexy."

She scowled and turned her attention back to the airship dropping into final approach.

Captain Vern O'Leary, the chief pilot of the operation, was flying. With familiar expertise he swung the ship's nose into the wind and it dove toward the ground. Just as it seemed as if he would drive the nose of the blimp into the asphalt of the runway, the giant airship swooped upward to level out. The engines roared as the dangling nose lines touched the ground and the linemen walked out in two lines, single file, toward the oncoming ship.

The passengers' smiling faces were visible in the windows of the gondola, watching as the crewmen grabbed the ropes. They snapped pictures excitedly as the ship settled into the landing, while all the time O'Leary explained exactly what was happening around them.

Lexy led her line, followed by K.C., then Kerry. Beside her, working in mirror-image movements, was the other line, made up of Red Riley, Sheldon Carr, and George Hanley. With practiced teamwork they grabbed the lines and immediately turned and ran outward from the airship to the side until the lines were extended.

Out in front of the airship, Killigrew, the crew chief, gave them the signal to slacken off when the airship was settled and no longer moving. The rest of the crew walked toward the gondola, positioning themselves around the handrail that ran around the bottom to control its movement while the crewmen on the ladder began taking the passengers off and helping the new passengers aboard.

Within two minutes the passenger exchange was finished and a whole new group of eight was ready to take off. O'Leary was already answering their questions about their once-in-a-lifetime experience. Lexy knew that the excitement and the enthusiasm was what kept all of the crew enjoying their jobs, from O'Leary and the other pilots through the ranks to the most junior crewman.

When O'Leary received the radio clearance from the airport tower, Killigrew gave the signal to "up-ship." The crew pushed the gondola upward. When it was clear of the ground and full control was again O'Leary's, Killigrew signaled the linemen to let go of the nose lines. Once more the *Andromeda* was free and in flight.

Lexy covered her ears with her hands as the engines roared, and she turned to walk back toward the mooring-mast area. A moment later Red Riley caught up with her, and when the engine roar had died off as the ship reached altitude, she took her hands off her ears to hear what he had to say.

"You ready for tomorrow?" His hazel eyes twinkled mischievously in his weather-beaten face.

"Okay, I'll bite, Red. What's tomorrow?"

"Cameron comes back."

Lexy groaned. "Cameron. Cameron. All I hear is Cameron. I almost feel as if I dislike him already."

Red laughed. "You won't dislike him, I guarantee you that. No woman does."

"It's just intuition, I guess, but I really have this gut feeling that I'm not going to like any man who once set the blimp crew record for the greatest number of one-night stands on a summer tour."

Red slapped her on the shoulder. "Honey, you'll love him. You won't be able to help yourself."

"Red, I have to work with him and I have to be polite to him, but I don't have to like him."

"You're just letting your women's-lib stubbornness get in the way. You'll see."

As they reached the mast area she said, "Red, if I

had to love any man on the face of this earth, I think your infamous Cameron would be the absolute last."

She heard snickers behind her as she realized several of the other crewmen had overheard her last comment. She shook her head. "Don't you just hate hero-worshipers?" she asked no one in particular.

Red took the jibe good-naturedly. "Hey, history counts. The man has what it takes." He made a rude gesture and the rest of the guys broke into laughter much to Lexy's dismay. She shook her head, hoping the slight blush that crept up her neck wasn't too visible.

Lexy endured the rowdy comments and recollections of the inestimable Cameron's exploits with the ladies as the crew went about the familiar process of raising the mooring mast and attaching the guy cables to the steel ground stakes.

Finally, as they finished Killigrew said, "Who knows, boys? Three years in Europe might have mellowed him out. Maybe he's lost his touch."

"Maybe he's down to just one woman a night," K.C. said.

"Maybe he wore himself out and he's being sent home a mere shadow of his former self," Lexy quipped.

"That shadow could still show you what for, kid," Red said to a chorus of laughs.

With the haughtiest air she could muster, Lexy replied, "I have no doubt that he shall never get the chance."

There was a moment of silence as Lexy untangled the power cable and the rip line. Killigrew walked past, carrying the wind sock over his shoulder like a hobo's pack. "Girl, you got to be the only woman I know who's always in a losing battle."

Lexy smiled at the grizzled, gray crew chief. "I

13

know, I know. I'm also the only woman you know who fits the size of her work boot to her mouth instead of her foot."

Killigrew walked on, following the rest of the crew, heading out onto the field toward their landing area. One comment floated back to Lexy that made Killigrew glance her way, his eyes sad. "She wouldn't have a chance. Cameron likes *feminine* women."

Lexy showed no reaction to the comment, but inside she felt a twinge. One thing she could never overcome was the recurring attitude among some of the men that she was less of a woman because she had chosen this career. By thirty, most of the women she knew were or had been married; many had children or were looking forward to them, and most of them had satisfying private lives.

Alone at the mast, Lexy leaned against the orange and white aluminum pole, wondering what she was really feeling. She decided she was confused, more than anything else. After all, the only men she really spent any time with anymore were the crewmen. She had to be careful lest she found her own standards reflecting those of the men around her.

Although not the most beautiful woman in the world, she knew she was no "Bow-wow," as K.C. was unkind enough to call women below his standards; yet, somehow the crew made her feel inept as a woman.

For three years she had done her job without any complaint from the bosses about her skill, attitude, or behavior, which was more than could be said for several of the men. Some of the crewmen's wives even approved of her—the final and most difficult accomplishment of all.

"Oh, who cares, anyway?" she said aloud as she turned to climb the mast, threading her way through the guy cables to stand on the narrow pegs at the masthead.

Once up on top she could see the landing clearly. The blimp lazily dropped to the runway and the linemen ran out to grab the noselines. Fanning out to the side, they hauled mightily while the rest of the crew hurried toward the gondola and wrestled the airship into control. The landing was a little more formidable this time, since the wind had come up. Lexy's shirt was plastered to her back by the wind, and her hair tickled softly against her forehead as she checked her footing on the pegs.

Slowly the crew walked the airship closer to the mooring mast, bringing the *Andromeda* within reach of Lexy, who leaned out to grasp the nose by the fitting on the right noseline.

In the last moments before mooring, Lexy's world narrowed from the giant airship to the six-inch nose-cone spindle and the hole in the cup on the masthead into which it had to slip squarely. With all of her strength she tugged the nose of the airship up the last few inches in spite of the wind pushing against it. "Come on, baby," she muttered, and at the last moment the spindle slipped into the mooring cup with a loud thump. Instantly, Lexy pulled the lever, locking it into place. She signaled that it was secure, and yelled to Killigrew, "Locked!"

Killigrew waved his arms in the all-clear. Then he glanced up to Lexy again as he said "Good job!" and immediately went about the rest of his duties without further acknowledgment.

Lexy smiled. Killigrew was not generous with his praise, so she felt pleased.

The crew busily attached the ground support equipment to the airship as Lexy checked the lock and safety on the mast. She climbed down just as the passengers from the last flight were walking away from the airship. Two attractive young women in their early twenties stared up at her openmouthed as she descended the mast. Lexy nodded politely and went about her duties with a mild feeling of satisfaction.

"Lexy, you've got first watch!" Killigrew yelled. "Set up the ship."

Lexy crossed to the gondola, where she clambered up the ladder into the cockpit. O'Leary had shut off most of the systems already, but she finished setting up the instruments for watch when she replaced him in the pilot's seat.

Within ten minutes everything was secured and Lexy climbed out of the airship to check the ballast. The ship floated slightly off the ground, so she grabbed a twenty-five pound ballast bag and tossed it into the ballast compartment. The landing gear touched the grass again. Killigrew said, "Looks good. The winds shouldn't get up above thirty-five, but call me at the hotel if they do, and I'll double the watch. Otherwise it's all yours."

The day was over for the rest of the crew. Lexy's would end at midnight, when Mark Randall came to relieve her. He would stay until six in the morning, when someone else would relieve him.

Lexy enjoyed her watches, the time alone with the airship, "baby-sitting"—checking the ballast and the pressure each hour, cleaning up the engines, or doing small duties. When all the duties were finished, she could read or watch the little portable TV in the truck, as long as she kept one eye on the airship and made the hourly checks. Usually the first watch after secure time was busy with visitors who walked out to see the airship. Lexy always enjoyed that part, talking about the airship to interested people.

Unfortunately, since Portland International was a restricted airport and not open to the general public beyond the airline terminal on the far side of the giant field, she did not expect any visitors to break up the hours of the watch.

The wind died off as the sun went down, so Lexy could relax a little. She had long since finished her duties on the airship, and decided to go back to the tractor-trailer to make coffee. As she trudged the hundred yards to the truck she saw a man walk past the front of the truck from the direction of the Horizon Air hangars a quarter mile away. She hurried to catch him before he went inside the semi's trailer, which he had no business entering.

"Please stop!" she yelled. "No one is allowed inside the truck."

He was halfway up the steps into the side door of the trailer. He looked surprised to see her, but she wasn't sure if it was merely because there was someone there to stop him or that she was a woman.

She noticed that the man wore street clothes, not the uniform of any airline or airport employee. His slacks were well-tailored tan corduroy, and his jacket was camel velveteen worn over a blue polo shirt. Closer, she irrelevantly thought how his shirt matched his eyes so perfectly. His black curly hair and black mustache gave him a rakish appearance. He smiled, flashing very white teeth and dimples. Dark hair curled at the neck of his shirt.

"Hello, there," he said. "Are you the guy—person —on watch?"

"Yes," she said. "Would you like a better look at the airship?"

"A better look?" His fascinating blue eyes met hers. "I think I would."

"I didn't mean to snap at you, but visitors are not

17

allowed inside, mainly for insurance reasons. I'm sure you understand. It's a mobile workshop and generator, and to someone not familiar with things, it might be hazardous."

"I understand," he said.

"Excuse me just a moment; I need a cup of coffee," Lexy said, stepping inside the semitrailer. "The wind was a little chilly out there." She took her cup from its hook on the wall over the workbench and dusted it out. When she noticed him watching her, she shrugged sheepishly. "On this job you get used to dust and stuff like that. Anyway, it's safe: The coffee is so bad it kills all the germs."

He chuckled with her. "Got another cup?"

"Sure." Lexy dug into the rigger's cabinet and found a package of cardboard cups, then poured him a cup of the steaming coffee from the drip machine on the workbench. "Cream or sugar?"

"Black," he said. "Good and strong."

"Strong, yes; good, I won't promise," Lexy told him, handing him his cup as she came down the steps. His hand brushed hers as he took the cup; it was as warm as his smile.

"You're the only woman here?" he asked.

"I'm the crewman on watch, if that's what you mean," Lexy said as they started toward the airship, which shifted lazily in the dusk breeze.

"I was watching the landing as I came across the airport. It looked a little dangerous. Doesn't that bother you?"

Lexy smiled. "I'll bet your next question is 'What's a nice girl like you doing in a place like this?'"

"Sorry if I sound a little nosy. I'm just curious about a woman who would take a job like this."

Lexy peered up at him. He was so tall, she thought. "I thought you were curious about the airship."

18

"Her too. I've seen blimps before, but you are a surprise."

Lexy noted his reference to *Andromeda* as "her," the recognition that she was a ship, a connection few laymen made. "Are you in aviation?"

He nodded. "I'm here in Portland on business."

The airship swung slowly toward them as they approached, and the short tail lines dangled and swayed toward their heads. Lexy batted one lightly aside and gazed upward at the gigantic shape over them.

"You really like the blimp, don't you?" he asked.

"It's the biggest thing in my life."

He smiled at her obvious joke. "Come on, here you are, the only woman among a whole crew of men—"

"Look, I'm not nearly as interesting as the airship."

"Oh, but you are." He smiled again. "I find women like you fascinating."

"What do you mean, 'women like me'? You make me sound like some sort of laboratory animal."

"I don't mean to," he said. "It's just that the women I've been around for a while are rather dull and old-fashioned—not willing to try something new."

They had reached the gondola, and he stood with his back to it as it shifted closer to them. Just as Lexy started to mention that he was about to be nudged by the airship shifting on its mooring, he stepped out of the way.

Lexy's hot coffee slopped over the rim of her cup, stinging her fingers. She welcomed the distraction. This tall blue-eyed man was bothering her. Usually people came out to see the airship and they talked about the blimp. They asked questions about the crew, but usually they were the kind of nonpersonal questions that were easily fielded. Something about this conversation was making her very uncomfortable.

"I don't even know your name, and you're asking me questions I won't answer for guys I've known for years," she said.

"Okay, Lexy," he said. "Short for"—he seemed to make a guess—"Alexandra?"

She looked surprised.

"I read your jacket," he said.

Lexy glanced down, so used to her uniform that she had forgotten her name was printed across her right breast pocket. "Okay," she said. "Who are you?"

"My name is Ramsay," he said as he stuck out his hand.

Lexy shook it with a warm, firm grip. "Don't tell me we'll exchange business cards next," she said dryly.

He laughed, a hearty sound that Lexy could not help but like—rich and masculine.

"Now, tell me, do you really like being the only woman among a bunch of roughneck men?"

Lexy took a deep, tolerant breath. Haughtily she said, "Ramsay, my crew is a disparate group of various ages who occasionally exhibit the strong male tendency toward sexism and stubbornness. However, they are far from roughnecks."

Ramsay stared as if in awe of her sudden professional tone. "Okay, what's an obviously well-educated woman like you doing chasing a blimp for a living?"

"You don't give up." Something suddenly occurred to her. "You're not a reporter, are you?"

"Why?"

20

"I hate people who answer questions with questions."

"You do?" He blinked innocently.

Lexy suppressed a frustrated scream. "Why am I letting this man talk to me like this?" she asked the airship.

"Because you have to be nice to the public: This is a PR job," he said smugly.

Lexy took a deep breath. "The airship is two hundred and thirty feet long and filled with helium, a nonflammable inert gas second only to hydrogen in lifting ability."

"Does your husband mind you working in a job like this?"

"Hydrogen is not desirable because of its flammability, so aptly demonstrated by the notorious *Hindenburg* disaster."

Ramsay laughed again. "I can see how you get along with the men you work with. You simply ignore them."

"Sometimes that's the most effective thing, Ramsay."

She watched as he finished his coffee, smacked his lips, and said, "Jeez, was that awful, just like you promised."

Lexy struggled to hide the smile that broke through.

He spotted the trash can under the mast and deposited the used cup in it. "You keep a pretty tidy operation here."

"We're proud of it. After all, as you pointed out, we're a PR operation. Our chief pilot, Captain O'Leary, is a spit-and-polish commander."

Ramsay nodded appreciatively. "Sometimes that kind is a pain, but things run more smoothly. Sloppy operations are run by lazy people."

21

"Our crew chief, Killigrew, has been around a long time. He's what you might call 'old school' too."

"Do you like working for him?"

"Follow his orders and you get along just fine. It's that way with most of the senior technical people. They know their stuff, so junior crewmen listen to them."

"Does it bother them to be working with a woman?"

"Is that all you think about?" Lexy asked.

"What?"

"Women."

Ramsay grinned. "Yeah. I love women."

"That's not what I meant."

"I'm sorry. It's just that I'm really curious. I haven't run across too many women in this field. There is a good chance I may be in a similar situation working with a woman in an all-male environment. I'm genuinely curious about what the pitfalls and problems are from a woman's point of view."

"You want to be prepared," Lexy said.

Ramsay nodded, following her as she crossed to the gondola and pulled some ballast off the ship to lighten it.

"You're sure you're not a reporter?"

"I promise I'm not a reporter."

"Okay," she said.

"Suspicious, aren't you?"

"I work with men all the time," Lexy replied sarcastically. "It almost makes me want to give up on men all together to hear how they talk among themselves."

She picked up the bags she had pulled out of the ballast compartment and, with one in each hand, walked back toward the mast. "I don't know if my situation can be likened to those of too many other women breaking into a man's field. Not too many women have to work and live with the same men constantly. We live in each other's vest pocket, so there is little privacy. What privacy I have I fight hard for."

"Like what?"

Lexy shrugged. "My personal life, personal habits. That sort of thing."

Ramsay nodded, saying nothing.

"Although I'm one of the crew, I keep myself a little separate. I'm not a snob; I'm just a woman. I'm not trying to be a man. I'm not trying to act like a man. I simply am a woman doing a job I really enjoy, one that happens to be done by men everywhere else and always has been."

Ramsay gnawed his lower lip thoughtfully. "You're not some kind of ultrafeminist trying to put men in their place?"

Lexy laughed. "If that's what you expect out of every woman in a man's job, you'd better wake up. Some women—most I know, anyway—are in the job for the *job*, and not for any other reason. They want the money, the challenge, the upward mobility, just like a man. It's the economics, in most cases."

Ramsay moaned. "Are you going to start quoting statistics?"

Lexy smiled, realizing how serious she had been sounding. "You asked. I answered."

"Point taken." Ramsay stuck his hands in his pockets. "You're not married, are you?"

Suddenly she wanted him to know. "No," she answered. "Never have been."

"Relationships must be hard to maintain, traveling the way you do. Does your boyfriend travel with you?"

Reluctantly, Lexy shook her head. Somehow she

23

felt this was none of his business, yet she wanted him to know for reasons she could not define. "He works back in LA."

"Isn't it hard, being away so much? Long-distance relationships have to be pretty solid."

Lexy nodded.

There was an awkward moment of silence between them; then Ramsay said, "He's a lucky man."

Lexy turned back to the airship, searching for something she could do to change the subject.

Dusk had almost faded to complete darkness. Lexy walked slowly across to the mast and flipped the switch on the mast lights. The small spotlights flared in the comfortable darkness. Lexy aimed them upward slightly so they reflected off the silvery skin of the airship, bathing the immediate area in a soft light.

She saw that Ramsay was watching her. The way the tall, attractive man fixed her with those pale blue eyes gave Lexy an odd feeling. It felt almost as though he could see inside her, into the sudden attack of loneliness she was experiencing.

"You still haven't found out much about the airship, and I don't know a thing about you, Ramsay," she said, breaking the silence.

"I'm not very interesting," he said. "I'm single; I'm traveling, like you are; and I'm especially fond of things that fly."

"You said you're in aviation." Lexy felt a bit more comfortable, now that the subject was away from her.

"I wanted to be a pilot for a while, a long time ago."

"How long will you be in Portland?"

"I'm staying until the weekend," he said. For a moment Lexy felt as if he were being evasive.

"How long are *you* staying?" he asked.

"We leave Saturday for Pasco, in eastern Washington. In all, we travel about six months of the year."

"You must get tired of being a gypsy," Ramsay said.

"Not me. I enjoy traveling." Lexy returned to the gondola to take some more ballast off, realizing he had neatly maneuvered the subject away from himself again. She decided to return the conversation to the airship, where it belonged. "The wind died down, the sun is gone, and the temperature is dropping. The helium, reduced in volume, has less lifting ability, and the ship becomes heavy. So, the ballast is taken off to compensate."

She went on to explain the principles of ballasting and the consequences of the ship being allowed to become too heavy or too light. Then she broke off. "I'll warn you, I can go on about the airship for hours."

"I'll listen for hours."

Lexy felt herself flush nervously. "Haven't you someplace you need to be? It's getting late."

"Are you trying to get rid of me?"

"I don't mean to seem inhospitable, Ramsay, but I have duties I must see to," she lied.

Ramsay's blue eyes shone in the light from the mast. His smile was gentle. "How about meeting me for a drink after you get off work? I'd like to talk to you some more."

Lexy shook her head. "No, thank you. I don't make a practice of meeting strange men in bars."

"I'm not strange; I'm perfectly normal."

Lexy smiled. "I don't make a practice of meeting any kind of man in a bar, strange or normal."

"I just thought it might be nice to get better acquainted." He slid his hands into his pockets and said, "I can understand. You probably get lots of guys out here. . . ."

Lexy stifled her impulse to explain that men simply did not pay attention to her when she was in uniform, that she rarely talked to men outside the crew, and, most of all, that she steered clear of men when she was alone after dark on watch. Instead all she said was "No, Ramsay, I don't—not the way you mean. But thank you for the implication. It's rather flattering."

"It was nice to meet you, Lexy," he said. "Talking with you was very informative. But remember, I did offer the chance to talk more."

Without saying anything more, he turned and disappeared. Lexy watched the tall, intriguing stranger until he walked into one of the Horizon Air hangars. The *peep* of the hour chime on her watch reminded her that it was time to make her check on the ship, which she did with an absentmindedness that surprised her when she discovered that she could not remember how many ballast bags were aboard. She recounted them and wrote in the correct number.

What was wrong with her? How could an absolute stranger affect her like this? She was tired, she decided. That was it. They had been on the road for nearly two months now, out of Los Angeles on tour. She had been away from friends and from Adam for two months. First they had taken the airship to Oakland, then to Sacramento and Stockton, then Fresno. Then they had doubled back north to stop in Eugene and Salem, Oregon, before coming to Portland two weeks ago. Saturday they would leave for Pasco, in the desert country of eastern Washington, with a stop in Yakima.

Travel, no matter how exciting and how enjoyable, got tiring after a while, and everyone felt the effects.

In another month, Lexy knew, tempers would grow short and silly things would set off disagreements between good friends. Hotels would become dull, and no kind of recreation would be relaxing enough. Near the end of the tour the only trip anyone looked forward to was the last hundred miles into Los Angeles.

However, usually within a few weeks, a restlessness would overcome the crew, and soon they would be grousing about how dull it was to be trapped in Los Angeles, and they would all be ready for the next trip. So it was, Lexy decided, with the "gypsy life."

That was what the stranger had called it, thinking back to their conversation. He wore no wedding ring on his strong tanned hand, she recalled, amused at herself for noticing. He was traveling on business, he had said. She wondered where he was staying.

She wondered about his smile, his blue eyes, and the physique under his jacket and blue polo shirt. Dense black hair had curled at the open neck of the shirt, and she wondered how far down his torso it ran.

"Good Lord," she said under her breath, shocked at all this wondering. Shaking her head, she flipped the switch on the mast spotlight and walked back toward the truck for another cup of coffee.

CHAPTER TWO

By the time Mark relieved Lexy on watch, she had drunk a whole pot of coffee and walked to and from the ship at least twenty times. Driving back to the motel in the operations van, she decided she didn't even want to stop at the twenty-four-hour coffee shop at the shopping center near the motel, and went directly to the Modoc Motel. She parked the van beside the crew bus in the lot and walked to her room.

Television was dull, and Lexy was too restless to read after she took her shower. Usually she could lose herself in a novel or an old movie, but neither one held a particular appeal to her this evening. Perhaps it was not a night of happily-ever-afters, she thought. Rarely was she overcome with motel-room fever, but tonight she had a terrible case of it.

It was nearly one o'clock, so the motel coffee shop would be closed. Besides, she wasn't hungry. Ordinarily, after an extremely long day she could slip into bed and sleep when she needed to, but not tonight.

Restlessly she paced the room for a few minutes more, then resigned herself to go down to the Cave Bar, which would be open until two. She'd have a glass of wine and watch the barges on the Columbia River, then come back and go to bed. It was too late to call any of her regular escorts, like Kerry or Red, who would usually go with her on a moment's notice. Anyway, tonight she had no desire for company.

Lexy slipped into her best pair of black denims and a fuzzy off-white scoop-necked sweater. She dug out a pair of earrings and struggled into them, then carefully made up her eyes and chose a dark rose lipstick that would set off her tanned face. She fluffed up her hair a bit, hoping the frizziness into which it exploded when unbraided would look stylish. Her rough hands were hopeless, but the Cave Bar was dark, and she wasn't going there to impress anyone.

A look in the mirror nearly made her chicken out. Her shoulders were too broad from lifting ballast on the job, her hair was too fuzzy, and her chest was too big. She felt like a call girl in the tight jeans. Reluctantly she slipped into her high heels, deciding as she looked in her mirror that at least her height made her look thinner.

Tucking her room key and some money into her jeans, Lexy left before she changed her mind. As she walked down the long corridor from her wing and through the lush Modoc Motel, she hoped she would not run into any of the guys. It was pretty late, even for the habitual partiers, so she had little to worry about on a quiet Tuesday night.

In the lobby she smiled at the desk clerk, a fresh-faced young man who looked twice at her. He had never seen her out of uniform and probably hadn't realized she was a woman.

The Cave Bar was almost empty, except for two older businessman types at one table. The barmaid, Sherry, who had frizzy hair like Lexy's, smiled a surprised greeting.

"Alone tonight?" she asked.

Lexy nodded. "Long day."

"Uh-oh," Sherry said. "Man troubles?"

The bartender, a slender woman with short-cropped black hair, shook her head. "With your job, that's all it could be."

Lexy smiled. "Not one of the guys I work with, though." She sat down, welcoming the friendly feminine confidantes. It was rare that she had any women to talk with.

The bartender placed a cocktail napkin in front of Lexy. "What'll you have? Tell Aunt Sylvia all about it."

"White wine," Lexy said. "There isn't much to tell, really. Some good-looking man came out to the airship tonight, and I didn't exactly know how to handle him when he showed some interest beyond the blimp. I keep thinking of him, and me with a perfectly decent man waiting for me in LA."

"From the way the crew talks about you when they're in here, you're practically a nun. We never even knew you had a boyfriend." Sylvia set the wine in front of her.

Lexy took a sip, savoring the tart, fruity flavor after all the coffee she had drunk. "He's a television newsman in LA. His name is Adam Jeffords. We've been seeing each other for about three and a half years."

"What's the problem, then?" Sherry asked.

"I've been feeling a little lost lately. I love my job; it's just that sometimes I feel like I'm some kind of creature—neither female nor male. I suppose it's an identity crisis of some sort."

"I don't blame you. All you see for months on end are men, men, men." Sylvia tossed a wet towel into the basket under the bar for emphasis.

Sherry leaned on the bar and crossed her arms thoughtfully. "You know, there are some women who wouldn't think that was so bad."

"I'm not in it for the men, I'm in it for the airship."

Sherry leaned closer conspiratorially. "Aren't there any you feel yourself looking at, you know, *differently?*"

Lexy laughed. "Come on, you've seen my crew."

"Hey, some aren't bad-looking. Like Kerry, for instance. Or Mark," Sylvia said.

"Oh, they're okay, but none of them have that spark, that special thing that makes you look at them differently, like there's something more inside to know, something that might be a little dangerous or a little exciting." Suddenly a pair of blue eyes set in a handsome face came to mind, and Lexy lost herself for a moment. That smile and those eyes, she decided, could certainly fan a spark to a flame.

She was pensive for a moment, trying to remember if there was ever a time Adam had had that spark. Their relationship had grown slowly, from a meeting at the TV studio when she had come to do some special effects for a TV-show pilot, to dating occasionally, through the challenge of getting the crew position on the blimp. When Vulcan hired Lexy as their first woman crewman, Adam wanted to arrange some publicity, but Lexy refused because she didn't want to be labeled a freak. She had taken the job because of her fascination with the airship, not for some cause. She also sensed that any kind of fuss over her position might start resentment and make her acceptance as a natural member of the crew much more difficult.

Lexy's instincts about the crew had been right. Not allowing Adam to make a big fuss about her with Channel 8 helped her credibility among the men. It showed she was there to work, not simply to prove a point.

Gradually, Adam became used to her strange hours, and her back-breaking work, for that was what it was in the beginning. Many were the dinners and parties she had to decline on the grounds she was too tired or had an early start time in the morning. Their dating consisted mostly of movies now and then, of bicycle riding, or walking along the Strand in Redondo Beach, near her home.

Lexy thought back, realizing that she could count on her fingers the number of times Adam had tried to make love to her in the last year and a half. When he had made love to her, she admitted ruefully, he had been nothing to write home to Mom about.

Idly she wondered about Ramsay, the stranger. She wondered about those full lips under his black mustache, what it would be like to have him kiss her gently on the neck, the hairs of his mustache tickling her as he trailed soft nibbles down the cord of her throat to the hollow of her shoulder. She toyed with a lock of her own hair, thinking of how soft the black curls at the neck of his shirt would be to her fingertips. His hand had been warm; would his whole skin be warm and velvety to the touch? His shoulders were wide, strong with the conditioning of a man used to hard work. What would it be like to have those strong arms encircle her?

Adam was a small man, soft from his desk job, tidy in a way that was almost prissy compared to Ramsay. Adam had never made love to her by overwhelming her or by seducing her. Adam had always been agreeable about it, discussing it, arranging it, as though it were another bicycling date or tennis. Adam was handsome, like most television newsmen, but he didn't have the masculine edge that Lexy longed for. He was comfortable but had no spark.

Nibbling on a pretzel, Lexy stared out the window at the Columbia River. The lights of a barge played across the waters. In the distance the Thunderbird

Motel-at-the-Quay was a riot of lights across the river. She knew it was a balmy night, just right for walking along the dock behind the motel. How much more perfect than on the arm of a handsome man, someone caring and strong, with a spark inside him.

Sherry, returning from serving the businessmen, leaned on the bar beside her. "Doesn't it bother you that you don't have a social life with these guys?"

Sylvia popped at Sherry's backside with the bar towel and said, "Sherry, that's none of your business." Apologetically she added to Lexy, "You guys are here for so long, weeks at a time, that we sort of get to know intimate details about people. You know how men talk to bartenders."

Lexy shrugged, still nibbling at a pretzel. "That's okay. Believe me"—she sighed—"I have nothing to hide."

"Sherry keeps herself pretty busy. I don't think she realizes that not all women have the appetite she does."

Lexy took another sip of wine. "I haven't thought much about my 'appetite' for a long time. I guess my job isn't the place for it."

"You really like that job, as dirty and rough as it is?"

"Oh, the guys play that up sometimes, I think. It's not so tough. But yes, I do like it. Working on the airship is special. Only about three hundred people in the world work on airships."

"And you're the only woman?"

Lexy nodded. "I don't know about the entire world, but I'm the only woman in the United States. I'm the first Vulcan has hired, although another company had one a few years ago."

"What happened to her? She get married and settle down like a good little girl?" Sylvia asked dryly.

"She's in Akron in airship engineering, I understand," Alexandra said. "But I don't know how she could give up the field to get kicked upstairs to an office."

Sherry was counting her tips. "Hey, Lexy, I'm off in a few minutes. Why don't you come with me to the Red Lion? The disco there is lots of fun, and maybe you can meet somebody with that spark. Forget that guy in LA."

"No, thanks, Sherry. Sitting here is about my speed for bars. I'm not exactly a ball of fire."

Sherry closed out her cash box, handing it to Sylvia. "Okay, hon. I sure can't figure you out. You're brave enough to chase that blimp, run around grabbing ropes, and dodge propellers, but you're afraid of meeting men."

"I think some of my buddies talk too much," Lexy said. "Give me some time, Sherry. Being a swinger is new to me. Besides, who knows? A man with a spark might walk in here tonight, and how would it be if I was somewhere else?"

Sherry bid them good night and disappeared out the door. Lexy watched her go with a tinge of envy. "I guess I should have learned how to do this at a much earlier age instead of running around, doing practical things."

Sylvia poured her another glass of wine, and Lexy shook her head. That made it three. "This is it for me, Sylvia. I'm a cheap drunk and I'm feeling a little tipsy right now. You don't want me swinging from the chandeliers, do you?"

"Just getting you loosened up for Prince Charming," Sylvia said with a wink. She nodded toward the door, and Lexy glanced across the bar. "Will you look at that hunk?"

Walking across the lobby was Ramsay, the stranger

from the airship. Through the smoked-glass windows that lined the Cave Bar, she could see he still wore the blue polo shirt that matched his eyes. He stopped across from the entrance for a moment, looking at something in the gift-shop window.

Panic gripped Lexy somewhere around her stomach. Her heart dropped to the level of her knees and she moaned, "Oh, no," and looked frantically around the bar. "Put my tab on my room, Sylvia. I've got to go."

"But what about meeting your Prince Charming?"

"I've met him."

"Coward."

"That's me. Bye, Sylvia," and with that, Lexy fled for the door leading out onto the pool deck. Ducking behind an evergreen bush, she watched as he walked into the Cave Bar and sat down. Sylvia poured him a beer. He nodded at her but seemed not to want to talk, so Sylvia moved away.

Lexy watched him, realizing that for the last few hours she had regretted allowing him to get away. She had been fantasizing about him, comparing him to Adam, and talking herself into an infatuation with him. Now, confronted with him once again, she was running.

She also knew, practically speaking, that Ramsay could never live up to the fantasy she had concocted in the last few hours. She crouched behind the bushes, watching him as if he were some kind of rare animal, one that she might never see again.

And Lexy sensed the safe thing to do would be to keep it that way.

He looked very tired. Unsmiling now, his jaw showed a sternness that she had not seen earlier. Shoulders slumped slightly, he toyed restlessly with his beer glass and napkin, staring off toward the river.

Lexy rose slowly in the bushes and stepped toward the door to return to the bar. Her heart hammered in her chest and her mouth was dry. She had sworn she would never do anything like this in her life: meet a strange man in a bar.

Then she saw Red Riley crossing the lobby toward the Cave Bar. Before anyone saw her, Lexy shrank back into the bushes again, searching for an escape route before she was seen.

For a moment she warred with herself. She was a woman of thirty, grown and free. She was not married to Adam. She had every right in the world to walk into a bar and talk to anyone she desired. It was no one's business—and so what if the crew knew?

Lexy knew at that moment that if she walked back into the Cave Bar to Ramsay, Red Riley would see her and the entire crew would know about it in full detail the next day. Lexy knew, too, how they talked about their barroom conquests. She knew what they really thought about the women they picked up in bars for one-night stands. And what else would they think? They were strangers who met in a strange town and would never see each other again.

With a last look at where Ramsay sat, and at Red Riley entering the Cave Bar, Lexy slunk into the evergreens and toward the door to the closest wing of the motel, where she took the long way back to her room, alone.

Later, as she lay in bed, she knew it was best she never saw the blue-eyed stranger again. With all the confusing reactions she was having, she probably would have been silly enough to be completely taken by him. And where would that leave her? Finally convinced by her own common sense, Lexy rolled over and went to sleep.

CHAPTER THREE

The alarm clock went off a moment before the telephone rang with her wake-up call. Lexy lay for a few seconds wishing the ringing would stop, but she knew that it would not: The Modoc Motel was too conscientious. Throwing the heavy bedspread and blankets away in one swift movement, she leaped up and scurried across the large motel room to the desk where the phone was buried under her navy blue uniform sweater.

"Yes, hello," she managed, shivering in the morning chill.

"This is your eight-o'clock wake-up call" came the disgustingly cheery voice at the other end.

"Thank you, I'm up."

"Have a nice day."

"Thanks," Lexy said, and hung up. She searched the room for her robe, which had fallen off the edge of the bed during the night. When she found it, she quickly put on the lace-trimmed lavender paisley robe. It was cut generously, made of a warm brushed cotton her mother had fashioned in the style of a Victorian wrapper. Once into it, she resented having to get up a little less.

Lexy moaned to herself as last night's escapade came back: She had actually resorted to hiding in bushes to avoid a man she would never see again.

How stupid could she be? Yet, as she went about getting ready for work, a pair of blue eyes came to mind, along with a warm smile and curly chest hair. Lexy shook her head to drive the thoughts away, and refused to allow herself to think about Ramsay any more.

Opening the draperies, she could see that the Oregon sky was blue and clear. Usually it rained more than it had on this trip to Portland.

She plugged in her hot-water pot for tea and headed for the bathroom to shower. Today there would be a nine-thirty bus time, and although she had plenty of time, she never liked to push her luck.

As Lexy crossed the parking lot of the Modoc Motel at Jantzen Beach, she wished she had put on her sweater instead of just carrying it. The breeze was cool and damp from the Columbia River, on the far side of the motel. She waved as she saw Brant Killigrew emerge from the opposite wing of the motel, where he and the members of the crew with more seniority stayed, in the better rooms. He carried a cardboard box under his arm, and as Lexy came closer she saw that it was mail from home.

She mock-panted at him. His grizzled face broke into a grin. "Is that for me or the mail, lady?"

"The mail, sweets. I wouldn't even pant after Tom Selleck at this hour of the morning," Lexy said, falling into step beside him.

Kerry Larson appeared from around the back of the bus, wiping his slender hands on a rag as he walked toward them. Seeing Lexy, he tossed the rag at her and she ducked.

"And good morning to you, Kerry," she said, and stuck her tongue out at him.

"It's morning. That's about all I can say," he muttered as he picked up the rag from where it had fallen behind Lexy. "Hey, Killigrew," he said, "bus is down another couple quarts. I think there's an oil leak somewhere, so I'm going to have to go over it today. I want to fix it before we leave for Pasco on Saturday."

"Okay, but if it looks like it's got to go in the shop, talk to O'Leary."

The bus door was open and George Hanley sat in the driver's seat, reading the newspaper *Columbia*. A photograph of the Vulcan Tire & Rubber Company blimp was on the front page, making a landing. "Hey, Lexy, they got your best side," he said, taking a swallow of steaming coffee from a cardboard cup.

Lexy glanced at the front page. In the photo her back was to the camera as she bent over to pick up some ballast. Some laughter came from other crewmen in the bus.

Lexy scowled at George and said, "You're rude, George, very rude. At least I *have* a best side." As she turned, her elbow nudged his arm and hot coffee spilled onto his pants. "Oh, George, I'm sorry," she said sarcastically. "Was it hot?"

The laughter dissolved to guffaws as Lexy turned to see several other Vulcan crewmen already in the bus.

"Morning, gentlemen." Lexy smiled and made her way down the narrow aisle of the bus toward the back. The rear half of the customized motor coach was outfitted with racks in which the crew and pilots hung their garment bags, coats, and uniform jackets. Along the length of the bus on each side was a storage area above their heads where each crewman had a sectioned-off area for small personal belongings. Into hers, midway back, Lexy threw her sweater and her clutch wallet. The paperback she carried went into the temporarily unused compartment next to hers; it was filled with her books.

"You realize that when Cameron gets here, you'll have to find someplace else for your library," said Roger Ames from the back of the bus. He sat at the desk across the back wall, filling out the previous day's pilot log, late again, as usual.

"Well, the illustrious Mr. Cameron isn't here yet, so my library is safe." Lexy moved to stand beside the handsome man. He was one of the pilots. "How's Tracy?"

"Never get involved with someone more than five years younger than you are. They're a whole 'nother generation." He shook his head ruefully.

"Not me," Lexy said. "Is she staying with you or going back to LA?"

Roger shrugged. "Right now I don't know. She isn't sure if she wants to make the trip to Pasco or go home. She says it's too long a drive and the weather's too hot."

"LA's farther. Did you point that out?"

"Women. Try to point things like that out to them."

"What am I, Roger? Chopped liver?"

"You're a crewman. You're not really a woman," Roger said as he went back to his work.

Lexy frowned, looking down at her uniform; it was identical to the uniforms of the other dozen crewmen who milled about in the bus aisle or lounged in the seats, waiting to go to work. The only difference was, as Red occasionally pointed out, she had bulges where the rest of them didn't.

"Thanks, Roger." Lexy turned to find a seat before George started his usual wild ride to the airport.

It was an unspoken custom that Lexy got her own seat, and the one left open was the third from the

41

front on the left. It was under her overhead compartment, on the theory that if her books overflowed, they'd fall on her head and no one else's. She planted herself with only casual good mornings to the rest of the crew that had come aboard, and stared out the window.

George fired up the bus and got the air conditioner circulating the air, which was becoming thick with cigarette smoke as various crewmen lit up. Lexy, one of the nonsmoking minority on the crew, leaned close to the air vent beside her seat to breathe. She stared at the slight reflection of herself in the glass. It was kind of hard to tell she was a woman sometimes, when she was wearing her plain aviator sunglasses and no lipstick or jewelry. Her hair was curly in the front, with bangs, braided in the back to keep it out of the way. Still, from a distance she looked little different than curly haired K.C. or Sheldon. Her uniform shirts were men's, and had to be ordered too big in the body to fit her ample chest, so she had them tailored a little. Her trousers were women's uniform pants, but of the same dark blue double-knit as the men's. Her boots were the heavy safety type, regulation black.

In the distance, getting out of a red Corvette, Lexy saw an attractive woman of about her age, of a similar well-endowed build, slightly taller than average. This woman's hair was stylish, her clothes the chic uniform of a businesswoman dressed in a dark linen skirt and blazer and a tasteful red-ruffled silk blouse. She carried a briefcase and wore red high heels.

Greeting her was a handsome man in a business suit. They shook hands and walked toward the motel lobby together.

Some of the crew had noticed her, too, and choice

comments speculating on her charms and business floated back to Lexy. She chose to shut them out.

For a moment she envied the young woman, stylish and attractive, in the glamorous world of business, in which she could wear beautiful clothes, meet charming, sophisticated men, and carry a briefcase.

As the couple disappeared into the motel lobby she looked down at her hands. That woman probably had time for a manicure once a week too. Lexy's hands were tanned and strong, the nails trimmed short. Her palms were tough, with spots darkened by calluses even though she wore heavy leather work gloves. The lines were deep, and several scars showed whiter against her skin. Lexy sighed, for these were not the hands of a chic, sophisticated career woman.

But no chic, sophisticated career woman she knew of could pick up a hundred pounds of ballast and run it to a wind-shifting blimp and hand it off. Nor could any charming debutante she knew manage to pick up one end of a ten-foot section of mooring mast and hand it up into the truck.

But, Lexy had to admit, most women wouldn't want to. Again she sighed.

Lexy had tried not to think about her tipsy, near-scandalous behavior last night—and about Ramsay. He'd probably like a woman in a red Corvette.

Across the aisle Mark smiled at her. "Heavy sigh."

Lexy shrugged. "I have to keep reminding myself that it's my choice that I'm here and not driving a red Corvette."

"Another identity crisis?"

Lexy nodded. Mark was twenty-three and had been with the crew only two years. Yet, he was wiser and brighter than most, and he and Lexy had become instant friends in spite of their age difference.

Red spoke up. "If you'd gussy yourself up and look like a girl, and trot yourself through the meat-market once in a while, you might find yourself with one of them young three-piece-suit types on your arm."

"No, thank you, Red. You can keep your meat-market. Bars are no place to meet someone you want to really get to know."

"Shoot, honey, we do it all the time."

"*You* might, Red," Lexy said, damning herself for her hypocrisy as she said it. "But *I* wouldn't be caught dead doing it." *Even though you almost caught me last night.*

In a way, Lexy decided, she owed Red a debt of gratitude. Had he not walked in when he had, she would have succumbed to her romantic fantasy and returned to the bar to pick up the blue-eyed Ramsay. The thought made her regard Red more kindly at the moment, for she felt he had saved her from making a complete idiot of herself.

Killigrew squeezed past the tall, lanky Red in the aisle, hanging on to the overhead rack as George pulled the bus out of the parking lot. "You need to find yourself some nice young stud and improve your disposition, Lexy. Make us all a little happier. Make you easier to live with."

"You'll just have to live with me the way I am, Killigrew. I'll leave the one-night stands and the morning-after quarterbacking to all you beer-drinking Casanovas," she said without rancor. It was an old conversation, and always ended the same.

"You're gonna end up a sour old spinster."

"My choice. Besides, I've got a boyfriend, remember?" Lexy said.

Killigrew shuffled through the armload of mail he had been distributing and dropped a letter in her lap. "A love letter from Mr. Right."

Red snorted. "If he was any kind of Mr. Right, he wouldn't let you have a job like this."

"That's why he's Mr. Right." Lexy tore open the letter from Adam Jeffords. It was written on the KGTR television station's letterhead. "He's progressive enough to let me do exactly what I choose to do. And if I choose to be a blimper, that's fine with him."

"I wouldn't want my girl traveling all over the West Coast, living in a bus with a bunch of men like us—uncouth, rude, crude . . ." Red began, but trailed off when he realized she wasn't paying attention.

Lexy's smile froze on her face. The words she was reading echoed just what Red was saying—not as directly, but closely:

After our phone conversation the other night, I realized that you actually prefer traveling all over in a bus with that bunch of redneck, crude, insensitive clods chasing that stupid blimp. You refuse to come back where you belong and carry on a normal relationship among your intellectual and educational peers. I see so little of you that I hardly know you, and we've grown further and further apart. You have no interest in helping me with my career or developing our relationship to where you could leave the blimp and marry me.

Since you're gone so much, it won't surprise you to know that I've been seeing another woman, the new anchorwoman on our five-o'clock segment. I think you'd like her if you met her. She's all the things in you I've admired and loved. But she's here and you're gone six months out of the year with your flying circus.

I'm sorry, Lexy. I've given it three and a half years. It's time you settled down, and since you won't, I have to bow out and let you have your blimp crew instead of me.

You won't make a choice, so I've made one for you.

With love,
Adam.

Lexy stared at the letter for a moment, at the neatly typed page in front of her. Adam's secretary's initials were at the bottom. He had dictated it to her. Lexy would have laughed, but the smile refused to come. She realized Red was saying something and she looked up at him.

"Is he going to take you away from all this?" Red asked.

Lexy swallowed, feeling a little foolish and confused. "No."

Across the aisle Mark nudged Red. "Hey, Red. You fix the tie-down on the electric blower cable for me yet?"

"Ah, I clean forgot about it, Mark." Red dropped into the seat beside him, oblivious to the fact that Mark was not even paying attention to him. Mark watched Lexy and she managed a tight-lipped nod of thanks.

She turned to look out the window as the bus careened off the interstate and onto Marine Drive, toward Portland International Airport.

Ten minutes later Lexy had a grip on herself, but she felt stunned and empty. Adam's letter was so unexpected, so unlike him. He had always been so easygoing and so matter-of-fact about their unusual life-style, in which they wouldn't see each other for months at a time when Lexy was out of Los Angeles, and for weeks at a time in Los Angeles, when their work schedules did not coincide. Adam was so warm and understanding that Lexy had nicknamed him "the Phil Donahue of the LA news networks."

He had been a bit distant lately, she had noticed, and they seemed to have less and less to talk about as she found little about the politics of television newsrooms to interest her, and he found her adventures with the blimp beyond his ken. Perhaps, Lexy

46

amended her thoughts, not the adventures with the blimp but the *crew*.

Adam had been fully prepared for a full-scale battle when Lexy became a crewman three years before. He expected the standard resistance and harassment from the exclusively male world of airships. Yet, it had never come—not in the conventional way—not with verbal abuse or sexist jokes or threats. Instead the men were reasonable and polite, distant and cool.

They had held their opinions to themselves and did their jobs, simply waiting patiently for Lexy to give up. Lexy fought hard to keep up in the beginning, but had come through—not as the best crewman ever, but not as the worst, either. She pulled her weight and didn't complain. She asked for no special privileges, and even brought with her some comforts, such as in the area of labor relations, which required that the company provide a portable toilet at every sight where they moored for more than twenty-four hours.

The sense of fair play and humor Lexy had acquired, working in the film industry on location shoots with almost all-male crews, stood her in good stead. Although the blimpers could be a little more direct and a little more crude than most men she'd known, they weren't cruel ogres or redneck boors. They were mostly a family of closely knit men doing a sometimes rough job, and they were very particular about their ranks. It had taken a year before someone played the first honest practical joke on her and called her "one of the guys."

Something Adam never understood from his tailored suits and plush offices was that what he saw as crude and disrespectful of her was actually acceptance into a very elite family, the very tight, very small world of airships.

The bus roared down the country lane leading to the back gate at the west end of the airport. George whipped the bus past a farmer on a tractor pulling a hay wagon and devastated a hanging limb of a weeping willow tree before bursting into a bright patch of sunlight. Lexy looked down the road to where she knew her consolation lay. There at the end of the lane, sitting in the grassy field beside the back runway, sat her airship, the *Andromeda.*

She was silver, almost blinding with the morning sun reflecting off her aluminized fabric skin. She drifted lazily in the morning wind, back and forth, rising a bit off the ground, held cone to the mast by her red nose. The gondola attached to her belly gleamed white, with her red engine pods on either side.

In the shade of the airship stood the crewman on watch, Deckard, surrounded by a group of schoolchildren and their teachers. He was busy carrying ballast while the group stood by, patiently waiting for attention.

"Oh, Lexy. Looks like you're up," Killigrew said.

"Hey," she said. "Roger, isn't it a pilot's job to give the guided tour?"

From the back of the bus Roger replied, "Not if the boss wants you to do it, old girl."

Hoots and laughter came from the rest of the crew. *Baby-sitting* and *woman's work* floated back to her, and she made a face at the guys in general. "Okay, okay. But when those little kids grow up and buy Vulcan tires and pay for your retirement benefits, just remember who left them with the shining impression of our blimp."

As George pulled up at the gate Sammy Florsheim,

the plump and dynamic PR man for the operation, stepped onto the bus. "Morning, everybody. Half-hour flights today. Chow is from two until three thirty, and, Lexy, would you take that tour of kids while we get ready for launch?"

"Yes, sir," Lexy replied, ignoring the snickers around her.

Sammy disappeared into a nearby motor home that was painted with the same colors and logo as their bus and the tractor trailer. It was the portable PR office for the operation, and like a circus advance man he would go on ahead of the operation, set up, and begin conducting business with the local district offices for the company, setting up the complimentary flights that were the Vulcan Tire & Rubber Company's greatest promotional tool.

A few minutes later Lexy stood among the fifth graders of West Side Elementary summer school and fielded their questions as the crew worked around them, preparing the ship for launching. She would much rather have been doing her share, but instead was stuck with the fifty-cent tour again. She had to tell herself it was because she was good at it, articulate and knowledgeable, and not just because she was a woman and the logical one to handle the kids.

"How many blimps are there?" someone asked.

"Right now, there are nine airships like this in the world. Four belong to Vulcan Tire & Rubber Company. One belongs to the English, an experimental craft, and the other four belong to our closest competitor, that *other* tire company."

Lexy continued. She could almost let her mind wander as she spoke, she had done this so often for so many groups of scouts and schoolkids and tours of elderly folks on field trips.

Soon, she was relieved to see Killigrew strapping

on his walkie-talkie and the crew dividing up along the handrail around the base of the gondola. "Prince," Killigrew shouted across the mast area. "You climb."

"That means it's time for me to go work, so I want all of you to stand right here and stay put. I've got to climb up there." Lexy pointed up the red-and-white-checked pole that dominated the area, to which the airship was attached by then with its nose over their heads. "I have to release the blimp so they can take it out into the field and launch it."

Lexy pulled on her battered work gloves and scrambled up the thirty-five feet to the masthead and the nose of the airship. She waited until Killigrew signaled from below, then she pulled the lever. Immediately the nose of the blimp backed away from the masthead.

In the distance Lexy could see the pattern of airliners waiting for takeoff from the terminal on the far side of the airport, hazy in the morning mists from the Columbia River, a mile away. The line of airplanes grew longer, as they had to wait while the *Andromeda* was set up for takeoff. It always amused Lexy that even at the largest of airports the airplanes had to hold while the airship took off. As with sailing vessels and power vessels, the slower and less maneuverable airship had the right-of-way even over 747s and military planes.

She stood atop the mast awhile longer, watching the airship position for takeoff. Although the *Andromeda* was fat and ungainly on the ground as she was being pulled and tugged about by the crewmen, she was still a beauty, and made it all worthwhile to Lexy. As the ship gleamed in the morning sunlight, Lexy knew that those career women could have their manicures and their high heels; they could meet with their three-piece suits carrying briefcases, and drive their red Corvettes. Adam could have his anchorwoman. All the calluses, the bruises, and the extra muscle in her shoulders was worth it when the airship coasted away from the masthead and Lexy could stand up there above everyone, watching as her ship rose majestically into the air to fly away, silver against the brilliant blue sky.

At that moment Lexy knew that nothing in the world could interfere. Nothing could be better than the life she led, and nothing would change it.

The operations van pulling up below the mast brought Lexy back. She climbed swiftly down the mast hand over hand and dropped the last few feet to the ground.

"Hello again," a man's voice called out to her.

Her heart dropped inside her and her breath caught in her throat. He stood behind her at the base of the mast. She whirled, eyes wide behind her sunglasses.

He wore the same navy blue and white uniform as she, but the name over the pocket was Cameron, not Ramsay.

"You!" she exclaimed. "You said your name was Ramsay. You pretended you knew nothing about the airship!"

"I wanted to see what you knew," he said. "And my name *is* Ramsay—Cameron Ramsay. I thought perhaps you realized it at first, but—"

"I don't care if your name is Moses," Lexy snapped. "That was a rotten thing to do."

He nodded in agreement. "You're right, it was. But—"

Lexy shouldered past him to pick up the power cable and continue her mast duties. Her good mood was shattered as she thought how foolish he had made her feel.

In the distance the approaching crew were calling out greetings. Hurriedly he said, "Look, how about that drink tonight?"

"Boy, you've got a lot of nerve," Lexy said through gritted teeth. "Everything I've heard about you certainly seems to be true."

Red Riley and Brant Killigrew were the first to greet Cameron, slapping him on the back and shaking his hand. "Welcome back to the operation, buddy," Killigrew said. "Where the hell you been?"

Lexy turned her back as the rest of the crew gathered around Cameron. Suddenly she felt someone grab her arm, and Red dragged her back into the circle of the crew.

"You met our woman?" Red asked. "We finally got integrated. She's just one of the guys."

"Yeah, she raises our consciousness," K.C. quipped.

"This is Alexandra Prince," Killigrew said. "Cameron Ramsay."

Cameron stuck out his hand. "Hi," he said innocently. "I've heard a lot about you."

Lexy stared a moment, puzzled. He was not letting on that they had already met—or had started off on the wrong foot. She took his hand in that warm, firm grasp once again. "You've got quite a reputation yourself." Her tone was cool.

"It'll be a pleasure working with you, I'm sure." He smiled.

There were some snickers and nudges from a couple of the guys. Behind Cameron, Lexy saw K.C. with a smirk that made her want to paste him one.

"I don't think *pleasure* is the proper word, Mr. Ramsay. But out of necessity we will get along, won't we?"

Cameron's expression hardened. "We'll see," he said.

CHAPTER FOUR

As the hours dragged by, the crewmen who knew Cameron Ramsay from the years before he had gone to Europe gathered around to swap old stories, laugh, and reminisce. The men he did not know used the other moments to get acquainted with Cameron, to see what kind of man they would be working with. He was accepted completely, immediately. He was good at his job, as everyone could see from the first landing when he went for a line, expertly flipping the rope with a supple wrist directly into the hand of the man behind him.

By the end of the day Lexy decided Cameron was only showing off. His jokes were inane, his conversation banal. He was arrogant, vain, and irritating.

Lexy was sitting in the bus, reading the same page of Jane Austen's *Pride and Prejudice* for the third time, when Brant Killigrew dropped into the seat across the aisle.

"You don't like him, do you?"

Lexy glanced up innocently. "Who?"

"'Who'?" he mocked her. "Come on, Lexy. What's the trouble?"

Lexy felt herself flush. "I'm withholding my opinions until I get to know him better."

"Withholding your opinions? I'm glad you're not sitting on the Supreme Court."

"Look, Brant. I just . . ." Lexy sighed. "Okay. I met him last night. He came out to the airship and spent a while talking. He acted like he was a stranger —pretended not to know anything about the blimp, or me, or anything. Then when I saw him this morning, I—"

"Got all ticked off."

"It was a rotten thing to do."

"Maybe he didn't do it on purpose. Maybe it just turned out that way."

She shook her head. "He had ample time during the conversation to tell me who he was. As a matter of fact, he was evasive when I asked him directly what he did for a living."

Killigrew studied her. "How long was he out here?"

"Long enough," Lexy said absently.

"Long enough for what?" Killigrew's eyes narrowed speculatively.

"Oh, no you don't. You know me. Don't go assuming. . . ."

Killigrew laughed. "I wasn't asking if you were messing around on your watch, Lexy. I know better than that. I'm just trying to figure out why you have such an aversion to a man you obviously spent quite a while with last night."

"Maybe it took a long conversation to find out that I don't like him."

"Or that you do."

Lexy tossed down her book in exasperation. "Look, Brant, I know your interest is for the sake of the harmony of the crew—"

"No, I'm being a nosy, interfering old—."

"—Okay. But don't start anything and don't make any assumptions. There's nothing on which to base them."

55

Killigrew's deeply lined face was intent on her for a few moments before, with mischief in his eyes, he nodded. "Since there's nothing between you two, then maybe you'd better start acting civil to the poor man." He rose to leave. "Time for the landing, so now is your chance."

Lexy knew that she had just been coaxed into following an order: Make peace or else. Killigrew did not like ultimatums or direct orders when it came to the relations on the crew. He liked to let people do what they wanted—as long as it was for the best. The decision to make peace with Cameron Ramsay was Lexy's. However, Lexy also knew that if she stubbornly refused to cooperate, Killigrew would find another way to convince her—and it wouldn't be as subtle.

Cameron came out of the truck as the crew started walking onto the field to meet the airship, which was still a silver speck over the Columbia River. Lexy fell into step beside him and searched for something to say.

"Is it good to be back in the States?"

"Yeah," he said.

They walked a few more steps in silence. "How many of the guys have you worked with before?"

"Five or six."

Lexy glanced back to Killigrew, who was walking a few steps behind them. She shook her head, feeling a tight knot of frustration rising in her chest.

"Is the European operation much different?"

"Yeah," he said in a disinterested voice.

"Okay," she said, "I get the message."

She looked up at him coldly from behind her sunglasses. He wore wire-rimmed mirror sunglasses that prevented her from seeing his eyes. She saw the reflection of her own face, mouth tight and jaw set in

56

anger. He said nothing more, and she dropped back to walk with Killigrew.

"Don't say I didn't try," she said to Killigrew, who frowned. Lexy walked on to her position.

A few yards away, in his line, Cameron stood with his back to her, amiably chatting with George as if there were nothing in the world bothering him. Of course, she amended, there wasn't. He didn't care that she had tried to make peace. Good, she thought, then neither did she.

She turned to stare impassively out at the airship, on its approach, and put her mind back on more important things—such as where she would eat dinner.

One more day was finished. Lexy stood on top of the mooring mast, awaiting the approach of the blimp from the last flight. The crew walked the *Andromeda* slowly toward the pole. Killigrew attached the pull-in line and signaled Red to take it out into the field. The cable hummed through the masthead, and Lexy fixed her eyes on Killigrew. She heard a burst of laughter from the men on the left line and glanced their way. K.C., Cameron, and George were all laughing about something. Killigrew shot them a look and they stifled the laughter. Irrationally, Lexy was convinced the joke was at her expense. She looked down again.

Cameron's attention was not on Killigrew but on Lexy atop the mast. She felt as if his eyes were fingers touching her on the back of her neck as she reached out to grasp the nose cone of the blimp and guide it into position. The nose of the ship rose a little, and Lexy pulled downward to realign the spindle with the hole into which it had to slip. At the last moment it slid in perfectly and she breathed a little prayer of thanks that she had not screwed up. Cameron had nothing to criticize.

Lexy climbed down as the last of the ground-support equipment was secured to the ship. She glanced around to see what was left to do and spotted the blower sleeve, a long canvas air channel used with the emergency blower system.

Lexy carried it across to the air scoop, where it had to be mounted on the attach point, almost four feet over her head. She always managed by standing on her tiptoes and pushing herself up to hook the sleeve frame on the air scoop, but this time she missed the first time and had to step aside nimbly to keep the frame from dropping on her head. It did not weigh much, but even its ten pounds was a lot to hold overhead for even the few moments it took to maneuver it into position. Lexy pushed it up to try again.

"Let a tall guy do it" came Cameron's voice. He took the frame out of her hands and fastened it with maddening accuracy on the attach point. Lexy turned on him, her anger sharp, but something made her pause. He was smiling—warily—as if he knew she was mad. "You do the short guy's end."

Lexy picked up the other end of the canvas sleeve and slid it onto the mouth of the emergency blower fan, where it hung on the outrigger at shoulder level. Her fingers felt like sausages as she fumbled with the catch. "Need a hand?" he asked.

"No," she snapped. Finally the catch fastened and the job was done.

"You're pretty good on top of the mast," Cameron ventured.

"Thanks," she said, and walked away. Lexy concentrated on not tripping over some ballast bags, which would have made the day perfect.

Lexy heard Red Riley say, "Tryin' to get on her good side, Cam?"

"Does she have one?" Cameron replied.

Lexy froze, turning to glare at him. Cameron winced and held out two fingers in front of him in a cross, as if warding off a vampire.

Around Cameron a couple of the crew laughed. Lexy's face flamed and she walked on toward the bus, her back straight, shoulders square. She peeled off her gloves in the bus, slinging them savagely into her overhead.

Perching on the desk at the back of the bus, she stared out the window toward the airship, where Red Riley, the first watch, was wiping down the engine cowlings. She deliberately ignored the rest of the crew as they made their way in and settled into their bus seats.

Deciding to continue reading her book on the ride back, Lexy moved back down the aisle to her usual seat. Naturally, of all the seats on the bus he could have taken, Cameron Ramsay was sitting in *her* seat. She ignored him, reaching into her overhead for her book.

"Nice scenery," she heard Cameron say, and when she pulled the book out she saw that he was gazing innocently out of the window. Deckard, K.C., and George were fighting smirks. Lexy walked to the back of the bus with as much dignity as she could muster.

As she sat down Lexy noticed that her middle button was missing, letting her shirt gape. She had not even realized she had snagged it. She always wore a T-shirt underneath, but it was the principle of the thing. Suddenly she felt like it was her first day at work all over again—with all the self-consciousness about her body, the scrutiny of her work, the feeling of being watched and mocked for her efforts.

The bus started up with a rumble and she held on to the edge of the desk with white knuckles to keep from sliding around.

How, she wondered, in one short day could one man ruin a perfectly good life the way Cameron had ruined hers?

CHAPTER FIVE

"I'm like John Wayne," Alexandra heard Cameron say. "I think it's okay for a woman to have a job—just as long as she has dinner on the table when *I* get home from work."

Lexy gritted her teeth and kept walking toward the landing, stepping up her pace to get out of earshot. She heard laughter, but she wouldn't let herself turn on them to argue about a woman's place.

The past three days had been bewildering and frustrating for Lexy. Her snit had ripened into anger, then had slipped slowly into depression. To compound it, no one seemed to care. Her usual friends on the crew avoided her, since she wasn't any fun, and that depressed her further. Even Mark, who was usually sympathetic, was now distant, as if afraid of incurring her wrath. The rest of the crew seemed intent upon deliberately saying and doing things to antagonize her, like a pack of hounds harrying a vixen.

To Lexy, the center of it was Cameron, arrogant and sarcastic. In an effort to impress him, some of the guys made jokes at her expense. Red, happily sexist, now with an ally, had dusted off his old woman's-place-is-in-the-home jokes. Even Killigrew had stepped back and taken a hands-off attitude, and told her flatly that he did not want to hear her complaints, since *she* wouldn't make peace with Cameron.

The day was gray as Lexy's mood, threatening rain. The predictions and the look of the sky told them it would not be severe. It seemed likely that the rain would be a mere drizzle, chilly and inconvenient.

Lexy lined up with Mark and K.C., staring out toward the misty horizon where Mount Rainier was cloaked in rain clouds. Idly she wondered which would get there first, the blimp or the rain. She hoped it was the blimp, because after they exchanged passengers, she would have time to get her rain boots and jacket out of her locker in the truck before she got wet. She hated being wet; a little dampness was not bad, but soaked clothes irritated her.

She smiled at the irony. After all, how could she get much grouchier than she was already?

"Hey, Lexy, you stopping for a beer with us tonight?" Mark asked.

She stared at him in surprise and bit back any sarcastic reply about being allowed to tag along. "I didn't know you guys were stopping—"

"Red's been talking about the Roadhouse. He and Sheldon rented a car and a bunch of us are going over."

"It's a saloon, Lexy," K.C. said. "A lot of unsavory types hang out there."

Mark shot him a dirty look. "Come on, Lexy. It'll give you a chance to relax, lighten up a little."

She realized that the last thing K.C. wanted to hear was Lexy agreeing to go. As her voice dripped with sincerity she said, "Thank you, Mark. Perhaps you're right: I need to unwind a little. I'd be delighted."

"I'll tell the butler to have the carriage waiting," K.C. said as they started walking out. "The princess will be slumming with us."

"Shut up, K.C.," Lexy snapped. "You're getting to be a royal pain yourself."

Mark laughed and K.C. muttered an obscenity under his breath as they trotted out toward the incoming blimp to grab the nose lines. Lexy ventured a glance at the other line as they hauled on the ropes to stop the forward momentum of the blimp, and she saw Cameron looking back at her. She averted her eyes to Killigrew's hand signals. When she glanced that way again, it was in time to see Cameron say something to George, who also looked Lexy's way and laughed.

A blossom of anger grew behind her eyes like a headache. "Hey, Mark, who all's going?" Lexy asked with forced lightness.

Beside her he replied without taking his eyes off Killigrew, "Me, you, Red, Sheldon, K.C., Cameron."

I'm not going to let him run me off, she thought.

Minutes later, as they released the lines and the *Andromeda* sailed over their heads, it started to sprinkle lightly.

The next landing was barely controlled chaos. The *Andromeda* picked up a coating of rainwater that added several hundred pounds to her weight. She came in fast, and on the wet grass the ship was virtually unstoppable.

The linemen grabbed the sodden ropes and threw themselves against the force of the moving blimp, only to find themselves being dragged across the slick grass like waterskiers. At the end of her line Lexy struggled for balance and to keep the excess rope from tangling around her legs as it whipped behind her. She played out the rope, sliding down to the end. As she looked down to check the rope she heard a whoop ahead of her. Suddenly the grass was hitting her in the belly and she was skittering along on the ground.

K.C. had slid into a stray pile of ballast bags lying in the field. Immediately behind him Mark fell over him and let go of the line. Lexy, not watching in that moment, was caught completely unaware and slammed into Mark, sending them both skidding across the grass, spewing water in a mass of arms and legs and rope.

"Help 'em out, guys," Killigrew shouted.

On the other line Cameron was skidding along on the ground, the rope between his legs, unable to get any traction on the wet grass. George was picking himself up ten feet behind and Deckard was skiing along as if he were behind a boat instead of trying to stop a rampaging blimp.

Four men broke from the gondola and fanned out to rescue the tumbling and rolling linemen on both sides. Chuckles at the absurdity of it all rumbled among the crew as the blimp finally slowed to a halt. Inside the gondola the passengers dissolved into laughter, and Roger, now that the landing was accomplished safely, said over the radio, "Hey, Killigrew, what's next in Clown Alley?"

Hiding his own smirk, Killigrew snarled at the crew, "All right, you clowns, they want to see your next act."

Lexy untangled herself from Mark while K.C. and the other two crewmen held the line. "You okay?" Mark asked as he climbed slowly to his feet.

Lexy nodded, rubbing her rear end. She looked across to the other line, where she saw Cameron wiping the mud off the seat of his pants and George limping to catch his place on the line again.

"Anybody hurt?" Killigrew bellowed over the roar of the engines.

"No," chorused the crewmen from each line.

"Good. Because you do that again, you *will* be. By me personally," Killigrew said.

Formation restored, the four extra crewmen trotted back to the gondola to help take the passengers off. The linemen stood self-consciously as the passengers snapped pictures and pointed and chuckled at the muddy, rain-soaked ground crew. With the new compliment of eight passengers aboard, the blimp rose once more into the gray and rainy sky.

Killigrew's radio crackled, and across the field the crew could hear Roger call the weather too dense to continue flying. O'Leary, at the radio in the motor home, said, "Killigrew, we're securing early. Put her on the mast." A chorus of whistles and cheers drowned out the rest of his orders.

"Maybe the day isn't so bad after all," said Lexy as she walked with Mark and picked weeds and mud off their uniforms. "At least we get out of here early."

"Gives us time for a couple more beers," Mark said.

"Sounds good to me," Cameron said from behind them. Mark and Lexy paused for him to catch up.

"That's some waterskiing technique you have there," Lexy said before she remembered she was angry with him.

"Oh, you mean my spread-eagle flare?" He grinned, flapping his arms in a fair imitation. K.C. fell into step with them.

"Well, Graceful," he said to Lexy, "think you can keep from falling down in the bar?"

Before Lexy could shoot him a reply, Cameron said, "Are you coming too?"

She nodded. "Got any objections?"

"I'd heard a rumor you didn't go into bars with strange men."

"You guys aren't strange—a little odd, maybe, but not strange."

"So you *do* drink with the boys," he said as they reached the bus.

"That's about all she does with boys," K.C. said as he bounded up the steps into the bus. Cameron hung back to let her go ahead. Almost under his breath she heard him say, "Too bad."

Art Guthrie, the assistant chief pilot, sat in the front seat beside the radios, making out some expense reports. He grinned as he saw Cameron. "I heard you were back, you old son of a gun," he said, sticking out a plump hand to Cameron.

"Bad penny and all that," Cameron said, shaking his hand. "Good to see you, Art." He indicated the expense papers. "Still milking the company for any and every stray cent you can?"

Art chuckled. "Are you still walking out of the bars with the best-looking women?"

Cameron shrugged. "How was your vacation?"

"I had more action than I knew what to do with. Those cruise ships are crawling with desperate women just waiting for easy guys. Next time you ought to take some time and go with me. I had to come back to work to get some rest. . . ."

Lexy had deliberately let her attention wander from Art Guthrie the moment he had mentioned women. She stared out the window, trying to concentrate on the prospect of a good time at the Roadhouse with the guys.

She was not happy to see Guthrie back from vacation. It had been a pleasant two weeks without him. He was popular with most of the men, but he got on Lexy's nerves. The pilot was ingratiating and occasionally funny; yet, he was one of the most subtly sexist men she had ever met. His sexism took the form of thinking he was put on the earth to please as many women as he could and that that was really all women needed. In another period of history he would have been called a rake and a libertine. Now he was simply considered a swinger.

Personally, Lexy could not see what women saw in him. Her eyes moved to where Art and Cameron still chatted to each other across the aisle. Art was of medium height, with thinning brown hair styled to make the most of what he still had. He and Cameron were about the same age, but Cameron looked much younger. She attributed the lines that creased Art's plump features to his dissipation, whereas Cameron's lines were from laughter and squinting his blue eyes in a thousand afternoon suns, waiting for an airship. Art struggled to keep his waist trim, eating health food during the days so he could indulge himself and his women with fine restaurants in the evenings. Cameron's body was muscular and hard, without an ounce of fat expanding his waist. Art's fleshy body had little body hair, whereas Cameron had that pelt of black curly hair showing starkly against the white of his uniform shirt. . . .

Lexy licked her lips and swallowed hard. What was she thinking? A pang of something akin to pain had started deep inside of her abdomen and expanded to fill her body. She could feel her breasts aching under the taut fabric of her shirt.

Impulsively she stood up as the bus got under way, moving back to her closet space to get her sweater. She was not cold; quite the contrary, she felt as if she was in a stiflingly hot room. She needed an excuse to move around, to break the spell her mind had woven over her body.

Vern O'Leary was rummaging among his hanging jackets in his area a few sections away, and one of the things he pulled out was a battered fisherman's canvas hat, perching it absurdly on his silver hair.

"Is that the new pilot's uniform hat?" she asked. She hoped her voice was normal. Gradually the odd twisted feeling inside her disappeared.

"For me it is, starting tomorrow," Vern said. His expression was eager, like a kid about to play hooky.

As the bus headed back to the hotel Lexy stood patiently and listened as Vern explained all about his upcoming fishing trip, his first long vacation in over a year. She did not envy him his responsibility and knew that he deserved a break from being ringmaster of his flying circus.

Wistfully he said, "I sure wish that Margaret could be here. She loves fishing."

"When does Marcie deliver?" Lexy asked. His daughter was on the verge of having another grandchild in St. Louis, and Margaret, his wife, was back east with her.

Vern chuckled. "What time is it?"

"How will you know when you have a new grandbaby, if you're somewhere in the wilds of Oregon?"

Sheepishly he admitted, "I'll call every night."

"Congratulations, Vern. Isn't this her third?" Cameron said from behind Lexy. As the bus careened around a corner Cameron braced himself with arms outstretched across the aisle behind her. Lexy was startled, for she had not heard him come up the aisle. To Lexy, Cameron explained, "I remember Marcie when she discovered boys."

An irrational thought sprang into Lexy's mind. She knew exactly how the girl had felt. Cameron's body was within inches of hers as he swayed gently with the movement of the bus. She wondered if he was as oblivious to her as he seemed, talking amiably with Vern while she stood aching in front of him. She could smell his nearness, even over the cigarette smoke and other sweaty bodies in the bus. She knew his was the faintly musky scent filling her mind, tightening her throat, parching her lips.

"She had a terrible crush on Cam when he first joined the operation. Used to follow him around with calf eyes all the time," Vern said, "until she caught him with another woman. She was all of eleven at the time."

Guthrie made his way down the aisle, his expense papers in his hand for Vern to sign. "Isn't that the usual way Cameron gets into trouble."

"What?" Cameron asked. His voice was suddenly tight, unhappy.

"Having one woman catch you with another. I remember that time in Spokane, with those twin sisters . . ."

Lexy felt as if she were being smothered in the hot, close aisle of the bus. She turned abruptly to escape, only to find Cameron's chest mere inches from her nose. Her eyes flew to his, startled and wide. Their eyes locked for a moment, and in that moment she knew that he could see every thought in her mind, as if her eyes were library windows.

"Excuse me," she said hoarsely, and ducked under his arm to stumble back to her seat.

As she sat down Art Guthrie muttered something to Cameron, to which he replied, "She's a crewman, Art. Come off it." Guthrie mumbled again, then laughed at his own joke.

Lexy stared out the window, gnawing sullenly on a knuckle. Damn, she thought. If she was going to make a fool of herself, why did it have to be over Cameron?

CHAPTER SIX

The Roadhouse was a workingman's bar. The decor was unpretentious, with a 1930's flavor. There was a pool table in a side room, and in back, near the restrooms and the back door, a couple of video games hummed and blinked. The bar ran the length of the narrow building, with a big-screen TV hanging from the ceiling in one corner. A poster advertised the Monday-Night Football Happy Hour Party.

The place was not crowded; the evening was still early. A snowy-haired, jowly bartender set out bottled beer for a couple of husky guys in coveralls at the bar. At a table along the wall several more men in jeans and plaid shirts sat eating peanuts and drinking beer from bottles.

The Vulcan blimp crewmen sat together near the back, swilling beer and swapping stories. The dark bar was comfortable, and unlike at the hotel bar, they knew they could get a little rowdy without embarrassment.

Alexandra stood at the bar, waiting for a refill of her glass of white wine. She was fielding some of the standard questions about the airship and their operation.

Sometimes people were too pushy, though well-meaning in their curiosity. Gus, the bartender, was soft-spoken and funny. Lexy felt comfortable talking to him.

"Where do new crewmen usually come from?" Gus asked.

"They're usually trained from the ranks of the part-time crewmen hired to work during the winter months, when we're at our home base. Blimpers are kind of particular about who they work with, so they pick the new guys out of the ones with initiative— those who show they care about the airship and want to put in the time a job like this requires."

Gus wiped up a spill on the redwood bar. "How long did it take them to decide to hire a woman?"

Lexy smiled slightly, not meeting his eyes. "A while." She never went into the details, since it was between her and the company and no one else's business. "The closed ranks are understandable, though. After all, the airship or another crewman's life could be at stake if someone couldn't perform. It's no wonder they're reluctant to accept new individuals who haven't proven themselves."

Lexy felt a presence behind her and turned to see Cameron standing a few feet away with an empty beer glass. He ordered a refill. Gus moved to fill the glass and Cameron said, "It's interesting to hear both sides of an issue from a woman. Most women only see the aggressive side, not the defensive side of radical change like sexual integration."

Lexy took a deep breath to hold her temper. "Nice of you to put it so diplomatically." Her smile was chilly. "I do try to keep an open mind."

Silence fell between them. Gus set Cameron's beer on the bar. Cameron nodded his thanks. "Well, crewman, why not come join your buddies. I'm beginning to think you're avoiding us."

Only you, Lexy thought.

71

To Gus, Cameron said, "Excuse us? Could you bring another glass of wine to the table? She's not keeping up."

Lexy did not move, so Cameron took her arm. Gus was looking on with a frown, sensing—as a good bartender could—the undercurrent between them.

"Come on, dear," Cameron said.

Lexy knew he had had several beers, although he didn't act drunk. He had an edge to him she didn't like, something she had seen when she had rebuffed him that first morning. She was uneasy as he led her to the table, but took the chair beside him that he offered her.

"Didn't you guys teach her to drink like a man, since she's got a man's job?"

Lexy said quietly, "I thought you had noticed by now: I'm not a man, I'm a woman."

Cameron's blue eyes locked with hers. "I noticed."

Red spoke up, breaking the spell. "Hey, Cam, go easy. She ain't much of a drinker."

Ignoring Red, Lexy said quietly, "Not only am I a woman, but I am also a crewman and have been for three years. I have nothing left to prove to anyone."

Oblivious to the uncomfortable stares they were getting from the rest of the guys, Cameron said, "Are you sure this is what you want to do for a career?"

Lexy looked away from him to the other men and smiled. "Hey, a woman would have to be crazy not to want to work with fifteen virile, handsome, sexy animals."

"Now, if you could just *find* those fifteen virile, handsome, sexy animals," Sheldon said. They laughed, all glad for the levity.

"What kind of initiation did she get, Sheldon?" Cameron asked the short, plump electronics specialist.

Sheldon raised his eyebrows in surprise. He seemed to sense that Cameron's mood had taken a bad turn. "We haven't had an initiation since the time we got K.C. up on the stage in Tijuana with that stripper."

Cameron stared into his beer. "For a woman crewman the initiation would have to be special." A malicious smile crept across his handsome face. "I'm surprised you guys haven't gotten together and held a tag-team mast party."

Lexy's hand connected to his face with a resounding slap that seemed to ring throughout the bar. The crewmen at the table sat stunned. Cameron stared straight ahead, also stunned. At the bar the two men in coveralls looked toward the little group and commented between themselves.

Lexy sat silently for a moment, her face burning with embarrassment at what she had done. She had never slapped a man in her life, having always found scathing words adequate defense. Her hand stung; she could imagine how his cheek felt. She struggled to maintain calm, looking around the table.

K.C.'s mouth hung open; Sheldon was practically bug-eyed. Red was scowling at her, and Mark was hiding a snicker behind his beer bottle.

"Cameron, I apologize. That was uncalled for—" Lexy began, but the two men in coveralls from the bar interrupted, looming at her elbow.

"You boys givin' this lady a bad time?" the bigger of the two big men asked. *Tex* was written on the grimy patch of his oily coveralls. A ten-inch monkey wrench stuck out of his breast pocket like a ball-point pen.

K.C. jumped up, fists clenched. "What's it to you?"

Red grabbed him by the back of the belt, pulling him back down into his chair. "Cool it, K.C."

The other grease monkey, whose coveralls said *Bill*, growled, "We don't like seein' ladies insulted." He was missing two front teeth.

Mark slid his chair away from the table, and Sheldon groaned softly as Cameron said without looking up, "She ain't no lady, she's a *crewman.*"

"You're beginning to sound like dialogue out of a bad movie, all of you. As for you, Cameron, I went through this a long time ago. That puts you three years behind. So why don't you sober up and *shut up!*"

To the grease monkeys Lexy said, "Thank you, gentlemen. I appreciate your concern, but I can fight my own fights."

"Ain't that nice," Bill said. "She's protecting them."

"I guess they got a woman on their crew to be their mommy."

Red was on his feet, his hamlike hands doubled up, ready to fight. To Lexy's right Cameron started to rise, but with a lightning swing Tex sucker-punched him. Cameron's lanky body catapulted across the table, upsetting it and knocking Sheldon and Mark away. Lexy rolled off her chair and out of the way as Red came across the table at Bill. Tex picked up Mark with one hand as K.C. leaped onto his back.

"Come on, guys, you know the rules about fighting," Sheldon yelled, backing into the corner under the big-screen TV.

Cameron struggled to his feet. Tex shook K.C. off like a dog shaking off a fly and dropped Mark to go after Cameron, who was more his size. Mark slid to the floor, unhurt but dazed.

Seeing Tex go after Cameron, Lexy picked up her chair and swung it at Tex's back. *Just like that bad movie I was talking about,* she thought. But unlike in the

74

movies the chair didn't break, and Tex merely turned to face her with an indulgent look.

"Please don't do that," he said politely.

Open-mouthed, Lexy gaped as Cameron punched Tex, who slammed back against the wall, his nose a red smear on his face.

"Are you all right?" Lexy demanded, wide-eyed.

"Lexy, get out of here!" Cameron snapped at her.

Red was down but coming up again, and Bill had K.C. by the throat up against the wall. K.C. was flailing feebly, his arms a foot too short to connect. Seeing K.C. in trouble, Lexy ignored Cameron and grabbed a beer bottle to pitch at the back of Bill's head. The bottle hit Bill, K.C. hit the floor, the house lights went on, and above it all Gus roared, "I just called the cops! It's up to you guys."

Sheldon and Mark grabbed K.C., and Red pointed at the back door. "That way!"

Cameron turned away from Tex, who was snuffling through his broken nose, staring down at his bloody front in amazement.

To Lexy, Cameron said, "I said get out of here!"

"After you," she yelled back at him, climbing over the fallen chairs and tables. Cameron was right behind her. At the doorway she paused to check out the damage and called to Gus, "We'll settle up, Gus. Sorry."

Gus nodded grumpily from the bar where he watched them go. "I trust you, kiddo. Take care of those guys, will ya?"

Lexy nodded and followed Cameron as he limped out the door.

At the rental car the six of them paused to get their breath and let their hearts catch up.

"Boy, did you get us in trouble, Lexy," K.C. said.

"*Me?*" Lexy stared at him, outraged.

75

"Get in the car, K.C.," Red ordered, "before I kick your butt."

"Everybody okay?" Lexy asked, peering at Cameron. He was sporting the beginnings of a fat lip beneath his dark mustache, and a nasty black eye. When she reached out to him, he shrugged her off and eased himself painfully into the backseat of the car. Sheldon was driving, so Lexy slid in beside him, and Mark sat beside her.

The ride back was nearly silent except for Red, who said, "K.C., if I hear you bragging about this, I'm personally going to inflict pain on your scrawny little body."

"Yeah, but we won, didn't we?" K.C. said smugly.

From the backseat there was a soft thud and K.C. groaned. "I told you, boy," Red muttered, and they drove on in silence.

Later, at the Modoc Motel, Lexy followed Cameron as he limped down the corridor ahead of her, favoring his right leg. She reached her room first, but before she went inside she said, "Cameron, do you want some ice or something? You seem to have taken the worst of it."

He walked the rest of the way to his door. "Yeah. Bring some ice." He entered his room without looking back.

Lexy shrugged. She had to give him the benefit of the pardon for the night. He had a right to be put out, she figured. After all, she had slapped him, and then a great big stranger had punched him. It had gone downhill from there.

A few minutes later she stood at Cameron's door, her ice bucket full. He had left the door slightly ajar, but she hesitated for a moment before going in. She had to admit the man had good reason to be hostile toward her: Slapping him had been uncalled for. Af-

76

ter all, the grease monkeys would never have inter-
fered had she not overreacted to the same kind of
thing she heard day in and day out from the other
guys.

Something made Cameron different. She reacted
to him differently, thought of him differently from
the way she thought of the other crewmen. Never
had she met a crewman who confused and angered
her so. Never had she met a man who, without saying
or doing anything out of the ordinary, could evoke
such a response in her. No other crewman—no, she
corrected herself, no other *man*—ever made her feel
as she did when she was around Cameron. All he had
to do was look at her or brush past her in the bus, and
she felt as if she as if being assaulted, as if her de-
fenses were under seige.

She felt that he refused to honor her boundaries,
the walls she set up as a woman among men. Everyone else ignored her femininity in an unspoken
truce. Femininity had no place on the line; out there
she was a crewman, just like Mark, K.C., or George.

Now, suddenly, here was a man who made her
think of herself as a woman and who reacted to her as
though she were a woman. It had no place there, she
told herself. It was not fair for him to make her feel
things she had not felt in a long time. It was not fair
of him to make her ache. . . .

"Are you going to stand out there all night or can I
have my ice?" came Cameron's low voice grumpily.

Lexy frowned, squaring her shoulders. She pushed
the door open and walked in bravely. The room was
dim, lit only by the bathroom light. Cameron stood
at the sink, running water over a towel.

Lexy's stomach knotted. Cameron had taken off
his blood-spotted uniform shirt and stood naked to
the waist in front of the mirror. She hastily stepped

past the bathroom door to the table near the bed, where she set down the ice bucket.

"Is there anything else you need?" she asked with careful nonchalance.

He came out of the bathroom, holding the damp towel to his lip. "I've never been hit by a woman before." He limped toward her, his battered face unreadable in the dim light.

"Maybe you deserved it a long time ago," she said. She instantly regretted having said it and added, "I'm sorry. You seem to bring out the worst in me."

"Remember, I owe you one," he said. She still could not tell if he was angry, threatening her, or merely kidding.

Lexy felt her temper pique again. "Look, I said I was sorry. If you think a good right cross will heal your ego, then go ahead."

"You have guts, I'll give you that. You never stop fighting." Cameron stepped close to her and Lexy tensed. He reached beyond her to the table and picked up a handful of ice, packing it in the towel. "You fight even when you don't have to."

His nearness was reviving that curious ache inside of her and she knew he knew it. A slight smile tugged at the corner of his battered mouth.

"If you mean the bar, I couldn't just stand by and let those two go at you guys without doing my share."

"Your share? You could have gotten hurt!"

"So could Mark or Sheldon or K.C. Or *you*, for that matter." She reached up to touch his eye where it was already discolored. "It was my fight too."

His smile was gentle, his tone softer, as he said, "You don't always have to fight." She pulled her fingers back as if his face were a hot stove.

"Yes I do," Lexy said. Her breath was tight in her chest. She brushed past him, heading for the door.

"Alexandra," Cameron said.

She paused at the door. He stood there wearing only his navy blue uniform pants. His eyes seemed to glow in the dim light, transfixing her. His shoulders were broad, his skin velvety tan. Black hair smothered his chest and crept all the way down to where it disappeared under his waistband behind his belt, the buckle dangling down to the tightly drawn creases in his pants front.

Right then, the hardest words in the English language for Lexy to say were "Good night, Cameron." But she said them anyway.

CHAPTER SEVEN

"You both know the rules about fighting. What the hell were you thinking about?"

Lexy and Cameron stood outside the bus the next morning as Art Guthrie paced up and down in front of them, hands clasped behind his back. The errant thought in Lexy's mind was that he looked like Charles Laughton doing Captain Bligh.

The rest of the crew was already out at the airship site across the field, preparing the *Andromeda* for the flight up the Columbia River Gorge to eastern Washington. Guthrie had somehow gotten wind of the fight in the bar the night before and was holding Lexy and Cameron accountable as the ringleaders of the brawl.

"We're a public relations operation, but this is not the kind of public relations we had in mind."

Lexy glanced at Cameron's battered face. He stood stoically enduring the chewing out—aching, cranky, and slightly hung over.

"And on top of it all, it was *you two!* Cameron"—Art paused in front of him, peering up into Cameron's sunglasses—"you never pulled this even in your salad days. What did they teach you in Europe?"

Cameron shrugged without saying anything.

Art turned to Lexy. "And you: You're setting one

80

hell of an example as a woman—out there brawling in a bar like you were one of the men."

Lexy's eyes widened and she gritted her teeth. For a moment it felt as if all the blood had drained from her face.

Guthrie sailed on, oblivious. "Anyway, the important thing is that none of you was caught. All I would have needed was to explain to the home office that I had to bail out six of my crew from the county jail before we could meet our schedule. That would just be terrific, wouldn't it? Vern goes on vacation and six hours later, half the crew is in jail."

Before Guthrie's hypebole increased, Lexy interrupted. "It was not that serious, Art."

"*You* might not think so. I hear you were the cause."

Cameron was still silent, but he was staring at Art in surprise.

"If you mean I was in the middle of it, yes, I was. The two men thought Cameron had said something out of line to me and took it upon themselves—"

Guthrie interrupted. "Did you?" he demanded of Cameron.

Cameron opened his mouth, but Lexy beat him to it. "We had already settled our differences."

Guthrie resumed his pacing.

"Both of you, I like peace and quiet on my operation, and I don't get it when there's bickering on my crew." He paused again in front of Lexy. "Three years and you've had a perfect record, Lexy. I can't understand it. And you know this is the exact thing that the company warned might happen." His tone became fatherly, patronizing. "What's come over you? I thought we were over any bad reactions to your being here quite a while back."

Lexy took a deep breath, livid. "I hardly think that it's *my* fault that five other crewmen—"

Guthrie shook his head sadly. "Lexy, please don't get upset and bring women's rights and all that nonsense into this. You can't fight every new crewman who comes along. You can't expect everyone to like working with you."

Cameron's mouth hung open in astonishment as he stood beside them, now more an onlooker than a participant. Lexy forgot that he was there, and her world now consisted only of Art Guthrie standing before her in his starched pilot's uniform, the wings on his pocket glittering in the morning sun, his expression beatific.

"Now, I think this discussion has gone on long enough. It's time to get the blimp launched, and we've got to get on the road. Why don't you two shake hands and stop this bickering? No more barroom brawls. Okay, Lexy?"

She stared at Guthrie, frozen, speechless. A thousand things sprang to her lips, but she knew nothing she could say overrode the fact that with Vern on vacation, he was the man in charge and had the last word. She could hold her tongue for two weeks, until Vern returned.

Cameron finally got a word in. "Look, Art, you can't blame Alexandra for what happened. I—"

"I know, Cam. She can't help it. It's that women's lib stuff."

"What?" The word was strangled as it came out of her, sounding almost like a squawk.

"I'll smooth things over with Killigrew, too, Cam. He'll understand. No need to mar your first week back with something like this," Guthrie continued.

Lexy's caution went with the wind that chilled her through her uniform shirt. "Art, you make any report you damned well please. I know the truth and so does everyone who was there." She shot Cameron a hard look. "And you wonder why I never stop fighting?" she asked Cameron, her voice low and choked. With that she turned back to the bus, stalking up the steps and inside.

"Lexy, wait—" Cameron called after her.

She heard Art say, "Let her go, Cam. It's that temper of hers. Always been easy to fuse, especially when anybody brings up women's lib."

"Art, it was *not* her fault. *I* caused it."

"Cam, I understand." Art slapped his back affectionately. "Your shoulders are broad. It won't hurt to make points with her. My money's on you." With a broad wink Guthrie walked away, leaving Cameron alone.

Gloves in hand, Lexy waited until Art was out of earshot before she came out of the bus. "How dare you let that fatuous slug blame me!"

"Lexy, I tried—"

"Women's lib stuff. That's all I hear. Anytime anything happens, it's my fault, because I'm a woman and I'm here. I thought they'd outgrown that stuff, and now you're here and I have to start all over again." She glared up at him, hands on hips. "Well, buster, hang on to your jockstrap. I've got news for you. *I*'m not the one who has to adjust. You do. And you'd better do it quick, or I'll personally ship your carcass back to Europe with first-class postage."

"You're right," he said. "I'm sorry."

"And don't patronize me, you male chauvinist hydrocephalic simian. Go play with your friendly floozies who want to hear your sweet nothings. Don't bother making points with me."

Slapping her work gloves against her leg, Lexy strode away past Killigrew as he approached.

83

"Holy Hanna, what did you do, boy? I've never seen her that mad, not ever. Not even when Red filled her rain boots with live snails."

Cameron shook his head. "I think I just got caught in the DMZ of the battle of the sexes."

"Guthrie sets her off like a rocket and he honestly can't figure out what he says that's wrong."

"She called him a fatuous slug."

Killigrew grinned. "I'd advise staying in the bomb shelter for at least a week. What did she call you?" They started walking toward the airship.

"Male chauvinist hydrocephalic simian."

Killigrew whistled. "Not only do I not know what it is, I can't pronounce it!"

"An ape with water on the brain," Cameron explained.

"That's only good for about a seven on the Lexy scale of ten. She didn't describe any body parts. Worst she's ever called me was only a four—bird-brained twit. I don't know if I should feel lucky or left out."

Cameron was silent, contemplating it. His eyes were fixed on Lexy's figure at the mast, preparing to climb.

Killigrew continued. "Lay low. She'll cool down. Then distract her. It's the way I handle Ginny. It works"—Killigrew shrugged ruefully—"sometimes."

"Sometimes?"

"She's a woman; what else can you do?"

"How *is* Ginny?" Cameron asked, deliberately changing the subject.

Lexy was tying off the pull-in line when Killigrew and Cameron walked past, talking amiably about Killigrew's wife as if nothing at all had happened. She turned her back on him as they passed, furious. It meant nothing to him that Guthrie blamed her for the fight and, above all, nothing to him that she never wanted to speak to him for the rest of their natural lives. Lexy didn't wait for the signal to climb, but went up the thirty-five-foot mast early, to stand above everything—the only place on the whole field she could be sure she would not have to deal with a man.

By noon she felt like talking to people again. The ride on the bus was quiet, with only a few of the crew aboard. The tractor trailer was ahead of the bus with two crewmen in the cab, and behind the bus was a caravan of a half dozen private cars. As long as they stayed with the caravan and within contact of the company vehicles, crewmen could ride with their families when they changed locations, so more of them traveled that way than in the bus. It made the bus less crowded, with only six crewmen aboard for the ten hours it would take them to travel to Pasco, Washington.

Lexy had not slept well the night before. After returning to her room from Cameron's she had immediately taken a long, hot shower, then washed her hair, and finally turned the spray to needle streams as cold as she could stand it. Once in bed she had tossed fitfully, thinking about the man in the room down the hall and the warm invitation in his voice.

She had wanted desperately to take that bruised face in her hands, smooth back the curly black hair that fell across his forehead and . . .

"Lexy, would you like a soda?" It was Cameron's voice, and something clenched inside of her under her belt.

How could she forgive him for this morning, for

selling her out as he had? How could she even speak to him?

But it was the ache inside her that answered, "Yes, thanks." Inside she groaned. *You're so easy.*

Cameron's smile was lopsided from his swollen lip. His dark mustache was fluffier on one side than the other. It was his eye that looked bad: Dark red streaks emphasized the creases underneath, the lower lid was swollen, and a purplish bruise had spread onto his cheekbone where Tex's fist had connected.

"Peace offering?" he said, handing her the icy, dripping can.

"I think we should talk about the shape of the table first," she replied, taking the can. Cameron grinned.

"Huh?" K.C. asked from where he listened across the aisle.

"You're too young, kid," Cameron said. It was clear he appreciated the now ancient history reference to the Paris Peace Talks over Vietnam. He turned back to Lexy, cutting K.C. out of the conversation before he weaseled in any further.

"I've got more in my cooler," Cameron said, "if you get thirsty later."

She nodded. "Thanks." She wondered if she should start a meaningful conversation with him to impress him with her wit and intelligence, to fascinate him with her rational philosophy on life, or to let the entire conversation die, since nothing that fell into any of those categories came to mind.

"You have quite a way with words," Cameron said. "Nobody's ever called me a male chauvinist hydrocephalic simian."

"Lately a lot of things have been happening to you that have never happened before," Lexy replied. She opened the soda and drank. After she swallowed she closed her eyes with a smile. "Thanks again. That's wonderful."

"A blimper with manners, education, and a creative way with the English language—I still haven't figured out why you're here," Cameron said.

"Why bother to figure it out? Why are you here? Why is Sheldon here? He could be teaching electronics at USC, but he gave that up. Roger turned down a slot as a co-pilot with Pan Am. A lot of the guys could be doing other things."

"Point taken."

"My turn for a question," she said. "Why'd you trick me the other night when you came out on my watch?"

Cameron shrugged. "I didn't lie."

"True, but you didn't tell me the truth, either."

"I guess you caught me off guard. Somehow you weren't exactly what I expected on this job."

"Let me guess: You expected me to look like a Valkyrie or an Amazon."

"A who?" K.C. asked.

"K.C., learn to read, then come back," Cameron said.

K.C. muttered an obscenity at him. Ignoring it, Cameron reached into one of the overheads and pulled out a dog-eared issue of a skin magazine. "Here—improve your mind," he said.

"What's eating you?" K.C. demanded.

"Why'd you tell Guthrie about the fight?" Cameron said quietly.

"I didn't—"

"Bull," Cameron replied, his voice even. He was not angry, Lexy noted, but more like a big brother talking to a nasty kid. "I saw you at breakfast."

"I thought he'd think it was funny, the way Lexy slapped you. I didn't think he'd chew you guys out."

"Guthrie's in charge while Vern's away, K.C. Unless he's changed in the last few years, when he gets a little power, he thinks he's—"

"Captain Bligh?" Lexy finished for him.

Cameron laughed. "Exactly."

"I didn't tell him hardly anything," K.C. whined.

"You told him enough," Cameron said. "Why couldn't you keep it among the crew?"

"He would have noticed your face," K.C. tried to rationalize what he had done.

"True," Lexy said. "That would have been hard to explain."

"I could always have told him another woman did it," Cameron said with irony in his voice. "Art believes that women are capable of anything."

"What about you? Is that your philosophy too?"

"So I have a little past." Cameron opened his hands as if pleading innocence.

"A *little* past!" K.C. said with a laugh. "Cam, if I had *your* experience, I'd be an old man already."

"You keep running off at the mouth, you won't make it to anywhere near old," Cameron told him sternly.

Lexy concentrated on her soda, trying to ignore the odd twinge she felt whenever she heard anything about Cameron's record with women.

To exorcise the demon, she met it head on. "You've established quite a reputation among the crew."

"It gets a little exaggerated."

"You still hold the record for the most one-night stands on a summer tour," she said.

Cameron shrugged. "Not that many."

"I heard it was forty-seven," K.C. piped up.

Cameron turned on him savagely. "K.C., can't you

88

keep your nose out of other people's conversations?"

K.C. slouched down in his seat in a sulk. "Sorry—didn't realize you were *operating*."

An alarm went off in Lexy's mind. "Operating? You don't think you're operating on me, do you?"

"Not in the sense you think. I just want to be friends. . . ."

"That's a new line, Cam," K.C. mumbled.

"I see," Lexy said, tossing her empty soda can unerringly in the wastebasket under Deckard's seat.

"Will you guys fight somewhere else?" came Deckard's cranky growl. "How the hell can a guy get any sleep?"

Sheldon called from the front, "Anybody want a rest stop?"

"I do. I need some air." Lexy leaned over to pull her work boots on over her bright purple socks. She took her time lacing them, until she saw Cameron's feet disappear down the aisle.

The bus, followed by the rest of the vehicles, rolled slowly off Interstate 80N into a rest area. Lexy made her way stoically to the front of the bus and stood waiting until Sheldon pulled the parking brake, then hit the door and strode briskly toward the ladies' room.

Farther up the Columbia River, the landscape gradually changed from the lush green of Oregon to the rocky brown canyons and golden hills of the high desert of eastern Washington. The crew lunched at a truck stop at The Dalles, then proceeded up the road to Biggs, where they crossed the bridge out of Oregon into Washington, then climbed a long hill past an eerily accurate replica of Stonehenge to the rolling farmland.

Lexy watched the unusual landmark until it disappeared out of sight behind the top of the hill, curious about how much it resembled the original and wished she could ask Cameron, who once talked of visiting Salisbury Plain. He had joined George in the truck, replacing Red as navigator; Red now rode in the bus. At first she felt an odd sense of relief from the tension of sitting mere feet away from Cameron all morning. Now, she missed him.

Cameron bothered Lexy, and the fact that he bothered her bothered her more. She had never allowed a man to disturb her, to disrupt her thinking processes and distract her this way. It was stupid, she decided. She was acting like a teenager with a first crush.

That he was attractive was undeniable. Physically he was a handsome man. Intellectually he had revealed himself as well read, well educated, and fascinated with life. He was well adjusted and seemed to hold the world about him in perspective. He was single, unattached, and unencumbered by previous wives or children. In short he was too good to be true.

Lexy felt the dilemma of the single woman over thirty, although to her it was not the same crisis it was for many of her female friends. The dilemma was that very few handsome, attractive, personable men in the same age group were available or unencumbered. Most were either gay or so spoiled by their single status that decent relationships were impossible.

Yet, here was a seemingly perfect man—not *perfect*, she corrected herself, but with all the qualifications any woman could desire. Why was he not taken, married, or divorced?

Was it his womanizing? Was he a sexual athlete, as the men described him? Was his masculinity wrapped up in his ability to make hearts flutter and bedroom doors open? All the evidence pointed to it.

With this swirling in her mind Lexy closed her eyes, finally drifting off to a fitful sleep. She awakened when the bus rolled off the interstate onto the highway leading into the tri-cities of Richland, Kennewick, and Pasco. It was odd to think of these desert cities as a major shipping center, but the number of barges and freighters visible on the wide river was evidence of how busy it was.

For a moment Cameron was far from her mind. Then her view of the Kennewick Bridge was obscured by the side of the red, white, and blue Vulcan airship operations truck roaring past. Lexy caught a glimpse of Cameron on the passenger side in the cab, and her thoughts jumbled again.

This was ridiculous. She was determined not to let him bother her anymore. Rising, she walked to the back of the bus to where the water jug sat and drew a paper cup of water. As she was walking back she saw Red and K.C. in close conversation, with Red making marks in a small spiral notebook.

"Getting up another betting pool, Red?" Lexy asked.

Almost guiltily he shut the book. "Yeah. Just a private bet with some of the guys. With all the talk about changing the schedule and sending us on up to Spokane, we're thinking of making up a pool," he said hastily, and for a moment Lexy wondered if he was not telling her the truth for some reason. K.C. sat across from him in wide-eyed innocence.

"Okay," Lexy said. "Let me know what you come up with; I might want in."

She went back to her seat and glanced back at the

pair huddled conspiratorially. K.C. handed Red a
ten-dollar bill. Lexy scowled. She hoped K.C. and
Red were not getting into something that could
cause them some grief.

CHAPTER EIGHT

The toughest part of setting the mooring mast up at Tri-Cities Airport was driving the five-foot-long steel stakes that held the cables for the mast. Everyone took turns on the jackhammer—two at a time at the hot, sweaty work. Lexy teamed up with George, and they stood together being shaken to their eyeteeth by the action of the electric hammer. Between the generator in the truck behind them and the rattle of the hammer, the noise was deafening. Lexy closed her eyes, gritted her teeth, and waited out her turn. It was at times like this that she really did wonder why she had chosen this career over the air-conditioned comfort of a special-film-effects lab.

Lexy opened her eyes to see Cameron standing across from her, watching her work, a long blade of dry grass drooping out of his bruised mouth. She could not see his eyes behind his sunglasses, but felt them fixed on her. The rest of the guys stood away from the noise in small knots, talking and smoking cigarettes, waiting until there was more work to be done.

It took Lexy a moment to realize what it was he was staring at, then realized it was her chest. She glanced down, afraid that her shirt was gaping open again. Nothing was out of the ordinary, except . . . She felt a flush creep up her face. The action of the jackhammer was making her breasts shimmy under her uniform shirt like twin bowls of Jell-O. It was a physical phenomenon that had been forgotten by the other men long ago as the newness had worn off.

A slow grin spread across his face, then he turned away. For a moment she thought he might comment to someone else about it, but he seemed happy to keep it to himself.

Lexy frowned at him disapprovingly, but he ignored her to join Mark and K.C., who were horsing around by the truck. The stake they were driving was finally deep enough in the hard soil, so George switched off the jackhammer, breathed an exaggerated sigh of relief, and called, "One of you other big, strong macho types want to take over for me? I'm done."

Red and Killigrew broke from the group to relieve Lexy and George on the last stake. As she walked past Cameron she said icily, "I'm glad you're so easily amused."

"I'm just a student of cause and effect. Physics was my college major, you know," he said piously. "The effect of motion on mass . . ."

Lexy walked on, frustrated with herself that he had once more managed to get to her.

After the airship was securely masted and the crew were ready to head for the hotel, Killigrew made the announcement that they were dreading: Someone would have to stay and put backup stakes in to reinforce the mast in case of strong winds or rainy weather. Groans accompanied the announcement that the stakes would be put in that night instead of the next day, as usual.

"Stake-driving party—any volunteers?" he asked. "Who are today's heroes?" A benevolent smile creased his worn face. "Okay, let's make it Prince, Ramsay, and Riley."

The rest of the crew stampeded for the bus, leaving Lexy, Cameron, and Red alone beside the stake driver.

Lexy heaved a sigh of resignation. "Okay, boys. Let's get it over with."

"Lexy, you hold the stakes while Cam and I handle the hammer," Red said.

"Aren't we going to take turns?" Lexy asked.

"It's safer this way."

"Safer?" Cameron asked.

"Yeah—nobody likes a woman driver." Red guffawed at his own wit.

Cameron and Lexy looked at each other, disgusted. Red's laughter died off as suddenly as it had started. Grumpily he muttered, "Well, *I* thought it was funny."

"You think the Three Stooges are high drama too," Lexy told him, picking up the first stake and holding it in place.

"Hey, let's not get nasty. I think the Three Stooges are great," Cameron said.

Lexy rolled her eyes heavenward. "O Lord, deliver me."

Red and Cameron swung the hammer up and Lexy fitted the head of the stake into the socket of the hammer. Then they proceeded.

An hour later she and Cameron leaned into the last stake while Red excused himself "to visit the flowers," as he put it.

Alone under the moored airship, which had shifted with the wind to cut off the late-afternoon sun and cast some shade on them, Lexy and Cameron stood shoulder to shoulder, arms shaking in rhythm with the vibrating jackhammer. She had relaxed after they

95

had started, forgetting Cameron's blatant appraisal of her earlier, but abruptly it came back. His hand slid off the switch and the jackhammer quit.

Cameron was looking down at her, a curious half smile on his lips. Sweat trickled down the side of his neck into the collar of his uniform shirt, which he had unbuttoned several stakes earlier. Silvery beads of sweat hung amid his chest hair, and his skin glistened wetly.

"What are you doing tonight?" he asked. His voice was husky, as if it were difficult to get the words out.

Lexy swallowed hard, stepping back to get away from the heat radiating from the overworked jackhammer—or was it from Cameron?

She numbly tugged off her gloves for something to do. She wiped at a trickle of sweat that itched along the side of her neck. Her own shirt was half unbuttoned, and her T-shirt was soaked with perspiration. Self-consciously she buttoned up in spite of the heat.

"I'm busy. I have a previous commitment."

"Oh."

Hastily she explained, "I have an errand to run."

He did not say "Some other time" as she wanted him to. He merely turned to reel up the electrical cord to the jackhammer. A moment went by and Lexy saw Red standing by the truck a hundred yards away, watching them, but she forgot it in the rest of the tidying-up duties.

Lexy finally gave up trying to find a bakery open at eight-thirty in the evening in Pasco, Kennewick, or Richland. She found a food store and purchased a white frosted sheet cake large enough to yield a piece for each crewman and pilot, and the colored frosting to decorate it. Ordinarily she did not go to unusual lengths to celebrate someone's birthday, but Mark had been a little depressed the last couple of days, and she thought it might cheer him up. He was the youngest crewman but one of the most responsible, carrying a big burden as one of the airship's mechanics. It was tough to be away from home, family, and girl friend on a birthday.

It had been hard to choose between Mark's birthday cake and Cameron's veiled invitation, but common sense reigned. She knew her reaction to Cameron was an attack of lust and the prospect of forbidden fruit.

Lexy rifled the grocery bag for a package of chocolate-chip cookies and gnawed contemplatively at one while she waited at a stop light. Cameron was a co-worker and off limits. A strict rule she had heard over and over again all her life was especially applicable there: *You don't get your meat where you get your bread.*

In spite of her feminist principles or rhetoric, Lexy frequently found herself living like a nineteenth-century virgin, conscious of the opinions, attitudes, and morality—double standard though it was—of the majority of the men around her.

"Men," Lexy muttered aloud, as though it were a curse. As the light changed a burly guy in a pickup truck honked impatiently at her. "Dear Lord, why did you make them so necessary?" she asked.

Sometimes she felt as if she were part of a very large family and all of her brothers were watching her every move, not because they cared about her so much, but simply because they were nosy.

And there she was, contemplating incest with brother Cameron. No matter how stupid it was to gamble her status with the crew—a position for which she had worked hard and long—she knew in her heart that she wanted Cameron Ramsay and that

97

the next time he made an overture to her, she would respond.

She parked the company van in the parking lot of the hotel by the bus and took the cake and the rest of the groceries into the hotel.

Lexy stood at the elevator outside the cocktail lounge trying not to look inside where she thought Cameron might be. Her best bet, she decided, was to avoid temptation and put off the inevitable.

She could see the full length of the bar, where George, Kerry, and Red were happily swilling beer. Red was talking to a voluptuous redhead dressed in a bright green blouse and tight white jeans, who was draping herself on him as George and Kerry looked on.

The elevator doors opened and Guthrie walked out, dressed to kill in his designer jeans and polo shirt, pudgy tummy on automatic suck-in. "Why don't you go in and try to catch something, Lexy?"

"You seem to be the one bent on catching something, Art," she replied in a nastily sweet tone, "but that's okay: I'm sure there's enough penicillin in eastern Washington." She stepped past him and let the elevator close before she frowned again. She had a headache from her inner conflict about Cameron and did not need to be reminded of the narrow line she treaded by the likes of Art Guthrie. Sure, she could go in the bar and pick up "something," but the next day she'd be branded with a big red letter for her trouble.

Lexy reached the safety of her room, put on some water for hot tea, and set about decorating Mark's birthday cake. She was relieved that she had not seen Cameron. She knew his room was somewhere on the same corridor with the rest of the crew, but had no idea where. Tomorrow the room lists would be posted, and she would check then—just to make sure that he was not too near and so she could know which room to avoid.

Lexy sat at the table across from her balcony door, sipping tea and playing with the squirt can of frosting, practicing on a couple of cookies. When she idly traced Cameron's name in pink frosting, Lexy knew she was doomed.

For a doomed woman she felt awfully good while she frosted Mark's birthday cake with pink frosting and blue letters. She drew a little blue airship and some clouds, but stopped short at the pink hearts. It would be too hard to explain on a mechanic's birthday cake.

Lexy's alarm went off at the same time her wake-up call came. It was six A.M., she was cheerily informed. Still tired from the long, hard day and evening out the night before, she groaned, burying her face back in the pillow for a few more moments.

She put on her two-piece string bikini, adjusting the drawstring cups over her full breasts. Then covering it with a gauze caftan. Last summer, when they had come through Pasco, she had learned to her delight that the indoor pool was rarely occupied early in the morning, and never by any of the crew.

In the peace and quiet she almost felt as though she were in her own private spa, pampered and princesslike. The pool was glistening clear aqua. The room was warm from the morning sun filtering through the louvered windows overhead along the eaves. Through the full-length smoked-glass windows, she could see that the outdoor pool was also empty. Only the gardeners were moving about the grounds before the sun got too hot.

Lexy slipped out of the cover-up, knowing that

through the smoked glass no one could see in. Steam swirled up from the whirlpool at the other end of the room, where the top of someone's head was visible over the edge of the tiles. She slid slowly into the cold water of the main pool, feeling a twinge of purely selfish irritation that her private spa had been invaded—by Cameron.

At her slight splash he turned and Lexy resisted the impulse to duck under the water.

"Good morning," he called with a smile.

Lexy paddled over to the edge of the pool nearest the whirlpool bath. "Hi," she said lamely across the three feet separating them.

"I thought I'd be the only one here this early," he said.

"Me too. Nice, isn't it?"

"Better now," he said.

Lexy hoisted herself up on the edge of the pool. "Soaking out a hangover?"

Cameron slid back down into the steamy gray-green foam. "Not this time. Getting rid of the first signs of old age."

"Don't talk to me about old; we're about the same age, you know."

"Then you do pretty good for an old broad." He grinned.

"Thanks," she said, splashing some cold water on him.

They were both quiet for a moment. "Did you get your errand done?" he asked.

She nodded. "What did you do? I checked the bar before I went upstairs last night, but the only ones were George, Red, and Kerry. They get a little rowdy sometimes. I'd hate to start another brawl."

"Too bad I missed you. I was in there for a while, but the conversation got a little monotonous—rating the women they've known . . ." He paused, and she knew he was being polite about the term *known*.

She said nothing, so he continued. "I ended up in the coffee shop, and Art Guthrie came in. So I had an illuminating conversation about women in his past." Cameron shifted around to face her fully. "Do these guys always talk about sex? Don't they read books or have hobbies?"

"Do I really hear this coming from you, with *your* reputation?" she said.

"My reputation—no one seems to believe I've turned over a new leaf."

"Oh?" Lexy clasped her arms around her knees, scrunching up to keep warm.

"Well, things do change a fella," he said. "Come in —you look cold."

Lexy pulled herself from the pool and eased slowly into the hot water of the whirlpool. It did feel good swirling around her legs, the bubbles beating at her back and hips.

Cameron was staring across at her, his bad eye puffy and discolored. It gave him a rakish look.

"Of course," he continued, "that doesn't mean I'm no longer interested in sex. Not by a long shot."

Self-consciously, Lexy slid in a little deeper, letting the water lap over her full breasts, which did not cooperate and floated slightly in the salty water.

"Don't hide your body," he said. "You know, I have trouble remembering you're just one of the guys."

"I think that's why we can't get along. I have the same problem. I haven't had a man look at me the way you do in years." Suddenly she was no longer shy.

"Come on," he said. "Surely guys—"

"Not the crew. You know the kid-sister routine. And I never really get to meet other men—"

"You have a boyfriend."

Lexy realized she had never told anyone Adam had dumped her. She shook her head and a strand of pinned up hair dangled down across her shoulder to trail wetly across her skin. "Not anymore. Adam threw me over for an anchorwoman; I got the letter the day you rejoined the crew."

"Sorry. Tough to take?"

She was unsure how to respond. She was happy to be free of Adam since she had discovered her feelings for Cameron, yet still felt the twinge of rejection.

He must have thought her lack of response was an answer, for he said, "I guess it's none of my business." What drove the last twinge about Adam away was Cameron adding, "I can't say that I'm unhappy."

Lexy stared at him, amazed. Her silence seemed to make him uncomfortable.

He continued, "Damn it, Lexy, you've been making me crazy since we met, with your jokes and your crazy temper—and your body." His eyes raked over her and she sank self-consciously into the foaming water. Chagrined, he added, "Hey, I'm human and it's been a while since . . . well . . . I fooled around."

She laughed. "You sound like a school kid. 'Fooled around.' What happened to that macho John Wayne kind of guy?"

"Did you like my macho bit?" He leaned back, letting his legs float in the warm water.

"I hated it."

"Good. You were supposed to."

"I was supposed to?" She could feel her irritation growing, bubbling like the whirlpool around them.

"Yeah," he said. "You're fun to aggravate. You get mad like a wet cat, all spit and claws."

"You're insufferable."

"I know," he said smugly. "Ticklish?"

His toes brushed her leg like little fish in a pond. Lexy drew away. "Only when I'm irritated, so watch yourself." The little fish tickled her knee.

That sweet ache was back and she let it flow into her abdomen, where it radiated between her legs. She was glad she was submerged. She felt the tightness of her nipples under her bikini top.

She let her own feet play around his legs in the water. The surging of the whirlpool pounded against her back, foaming up under her arms to caress her breasts as if they were being touched by invisible hands.

She felt one of his feet against the inside of her thigh. He was just far enough away that he could reach no farther.

"Come over here—let me rub your shoulders," he said. "Few things feel better than a back rub in a whirlpool."

Lexy obeyed gladly. They both knew it was an excuse to get closer, to touch. He spread his legs and pulled her to sit between so he could massage her muscular arms and shoulders. The action of the water moved her gently against him, her buttocks firmly up against him.

"I like your shoulders—so strong and firm. Soft women feel so breakable," he murmured into her ear. His strong hands kneaded and pulled at her neck, moving farther and farther forward with each kneading motion. Her breasts ached to be touched.

Lexy heard herself moan softly. Then his arms slipped under hers and around to cup her swollen breasts. Her flesh overflowed the black fabric of her top and his fingers clutched at her almost painfully at first, then gently, lovingly.

Cameron's mouth fell against the hollow of her neck, his lips trailing warm kisses up to her ear, and just as she had imagined that first night they had met, his mustache tickled.

Her hips twisted against the hardness of his groin. She felt a spasm deep inside herself, as if something in her were trying to reach out to capture him, to draw him inside. She twisted to face him, meeting his mouth with hers.

Heedless of his tender lip, he crushed his mouth down on hers. They sank lower into the water, stretched full length along the tile seat. One of his sinewy arms kept them from slipping completely under the foaming, pulsating water.

"What if someone comes in?" Lexy whispered.

"We'll fake it," Cameron mumbled, kissing her again. "No one can see in, and we'd hear them coming."

One hand slipped her top up, freeing her breasts in the water. He pulled her up to bury his face between them. "I've been wanting to do this ever since I first saw you. You shouldn't hide them; they're beautiful," he said looking up with a mischievous smile. "And you can't hide them. Not from me."

He nibbled hungrily at the large rosy nipple, erect and tight. "I need you, but only if you want it too. I hoped to seduce you with candlelight and wine and soft music—"

"Later for that. I want you—right now," she demanded. The ache was too great, the need too long unsatisfied. Her voice was like someone else's, another Alexandra—and she didn't care.

Under the cover of the water she untied one of the

104

strings to her bikini bottom and it drifted aside, freeing the mound of dark curls it hid.

Cameron's trunks were loose, jogger's nylon shorts that came off easily. He smiled gently. "Only if you want."

She nodded.

He sat back against the edge of the pool and swung her across his lap, facing him. She felt light, bobbing in the whirlpool, like a child on a swing. His hands gripped the tight spheres of her buttocks and drew her forward. She braced her arms on either side of his head. Her breasts pressed against the black forest of hair on his chest softly, ticklingly.

His blue eyes fixed hers with an almost wistful stare and he pulled her down to meet him.

Lexy felt him close to her. His eyes glazed and he groaned her name.

He filled her aching emptiness, sliding deeper and deeper until she thought he had no end—and wanted him to have no end.

"Slowly," she said. "Slowly . . ."

His expression was lost between astonishment and ecstasy as he bent to kiss first one breast, then the other, and finally, her mouth, biting at her lips, caressing her tongue with his.

The heat became unbearable, inside and out. Lexy moved on him, feeling him push against her so far that she was at the edge of pain, yet not quite, his hands on her, caressing, moving, the heat of the water fusing them in the surging rhythm of the foam.

It began like a wave that grew. In a voice tiny with awe and surprise Lexy said "Oh, Cam" and laid her head along his neck as she felt herself melt against him.

"Hold on," he whispered and thrust against her

more quickly, yet still with tortuous restraint. "I can't stop. . . ."

As she felt the wave engulf her from within, he tensed and pulled her tightly against him as together they surged and shuddered with the wild action of the water in the pool.

Clinging like shipwrecked mariners, they fell against the edge of the whirlpool in each other's arms, mouths barely touching, breaths heavy and mingling.

Their eyes met and he blinked, dazed, and moved one shaky hand to smooth back the fall of her wet curls across her damp forehead. She kissed him passionately.

At the same moment they looked around like a pair of guilty children to make sure they had no audience. Outside the smoked-glass windows, an old man dug at a bush with a hoe, back turned, oblivious. A few people now splashed in the outdoor pool beyond, but Cameron and Lexy were alone in each other's arms.

They had nothing to say, but held each other until their bodies ebbed and the heat of the whirlpool, still bubbling away around them, forced them to part.

Lexy tugged her bra top back into place, turning slightly as she had to adjust her breasts within the wet fabric. Cameron chuckled. "Embarrassed?"

"I shouldn't be—not now," she said.

"Never," he said, and leaned over to plant a kiss on the mound of one, then licked a drop of water from her chin before kissing her.

Both fumbled around to replace their swimsuit bottoms and at the same time started laughing.

"Sex is so silly," Lexy said. "Afterward, all the unromantic nonsense you go through."

Cameron agreed, hoisting himself out of the water to sit on the edge of the tiles.

"No regrets?" he said, wiping away the moisture from his mustache.

She shook her head.

"Does this change things at work?" he asked.

"Work and off time are two different places. I won't carry it over," she said. "And I hope you won't."

Behind them the pool room door opened and three little boys came hurrying in, each anxious to be the first in the water. Cameron rolled his eyes heavenward. "Nick of time, my dear."

Lexy continued, "I can only pray you're not the kind of man who kisses and tells."

"In case you're worried," he said, his tone a little harder, "I won't throw you to the wolves."

"I'm sorry. It's just—"

"Don't worry about it." Cameron extended a hand to help her out of the pool. She checked all her fastenings, then stepped up, taking his hand. "If anything else, I'd be damned ungrateful betraying you. Not to mention spoiling one of the best moments in my entire life."

It was then her eyes fixed on his right knee. A parallel set of scars ran like railroad tracks up either side, ugly and scarlet from the water.

"You know my secret, I know yours," he said.

She peered up at him, curious. "What secret?"

"I know that you're a wanton hussy, beautiful in the throes of passion."

Lexy groaned. "Don't tell me you wax poetical in your libidinous interludes."

"No more purple prose than you," he said.

They sat down in a couple of the patio chairs, toweling their upper bodies.

107

"And your secret—what's so secret about it?" she asked.

Cameron fingered the scars. "A year ago I had to have that done in Switzerland. It's roughly the same thing that happens to football players who get hit in the knees too often. I had one too many rough landings. The doctors didn't think I ought to continue chasing a blimp for a living."

"Why do you?"

"Didn't we have this conversation once? It gets to you, the helium bug. Basically I'll do it as long as the knee holds out."

Something inside Lexy twisted in the area of her heart. "You won't be with us too much longer, will you?"

"I don't know how long. It could be years." Then he added, "I'm okay, Lexy. Don't get too concerned."

Bravely she said, "I won't. You're a big boy. You know what you're doing."

"How about breakfast? I'm starved. I always feel hungry after I"—he paused—"spend time in the whirlpool."

"A lot of the guys will be in the restaurant by now."

"I forgot. I guess we still haven't really made up in public, have we?"

"You're still an insufferable, arrogant boor," she said matter-of-factly.

"Headstrong women's libber," he replied.

"Sounds like a good war."

Lexy rose to go get her cover-up. He caught her hand. "May I visit you tonight?"

"Just so no one sees you."

Mischievously he grinned. "Don't worry. I'll think of a way."

CHAPTER NINE

Later, as Lexy walked onto the bus, she reminded herself that she was an adult woman able to make her own choices and had no one to answer to. The purely physical encounter hours earlier in the whirlpool was over; it was a release of tension, passion, and frustration. If Cameron could not treat it as such, it would be his problem. With this very rational thought Lexy wondered why her stomach lurched and her throat constricted when she saw Cameron slouched comfortably in the seat across the aisle. He glanced up at her and smiled politely as she sat down in her customary seat.

Was he that indifferent?

She ventured a glance across at him. He yawned and stretched, looking bored. The other crewmen on the bus were busy reading or talking among themselves. With no one paying either of them any attention, Cameron winked at her, then slipped on his sunglasses.

Hiding a smile, Lexy turned to look out the window. It was going to be an interesting day.

She had hidden Mark's cake in one of the cabinets in the desk earlier that morning and waited until everyone was off the bus when they arrived at the airship site before she brought it out. Mark had gone out earlier in the company van for the preflight inspection, so he was already at the site.

At the mast Killigrew called everyone together, then summoned Mark from where he was studiously making some entries in the maintenance log while seated on the mechanic's equipment box. Mark's eyes were tired, his expression preoccupied as he approached, completely oblivious to the impending surprise. Of course, most of the crew were as ignorant of the reason for the gathering, and their surprise was as genuine as Mark's when Lexy stepped from behind Killigrew with the decorated cake in her hands.

Mark was speechless, and the rest of the crew broke into a ragged version of "Happy Birthday" with an added obscene verse at the end. Mark shuffled and gulped and said, "I guess I'd better put this in the bus before it gets all dusty; we'll eat it later." He hurried toward the bus while the rest of the crew moved into their regular duties to prepare the airship for launch.

It was after Killigrew commented on Lexy's thoughtfulness that she noticed Cameron watching with a strangely pensive expression.

After the launch they walked back toward the bus. Cameron caught up to her. "Was that your errand last night?"

"Alexandra Prince, mother hen," she said.

"You really care about these guys, don't you?"

She nodded. "It's like having a very large family. Mark is the little brother I never had."

Cameron grinned and said quietly, "What does that make me?"

"You're adopted, remember?" Lexy quipped and then hurried on before Red or K.C., who were walking a few yards ahead, overheard. Behind her Cameron laughed. She knew she had been right; it was turning out to be an interesting day.

Actually it was an interminable day. The temperature hovered in the high nineties. Florsheim had scheduled half-hour flights, which meant that every twenty-five minutes the crew stood out in the sun for a landing. Whirlwinds swirled dust in their eyes and sent the airship pitching and swinging wildly during landings. By noon everyone was irritable and exhausted, and the day was only half over.

Lexy and Cameron were working opposite lines as usual, although she wished she had chosen to work on his. Of course, changing her routine might make others suspicious so she had thought better of it. K.C. was prattling on about the "chick" in the bar last night putting the moves on Red so heatedly because she wanted a blimp ride. Lexy did not have to shut him up; Kerry did it for her by threatening to tell some girl K.C. had just met that he was under age.

The day wore on.

About four o'clock the slight wind had died and conditions became dangerous. Large whirlwinds, several hundred yards across, blew wildly over the airport, tugging at the light planes tied down a half mile away near the hangars, and raising clouds of dust on the sparse brown infield between runways.

It was during a landing that a whirlwind came out of nowhere, sucking the tail of the *Andromeda* around in passing. The blimp pivoted and the crew fought to control her. On their line, trying to hold the movement, Lexy, Kerry, and K.C. dug their heels into the sandy ground while the other line tried to outrun the shifting ship. Roger was piloting and signaled Killigrew to let the ship go: The safest thing was to get airborne and away from the giant dust devil.

The linemen threw aside their ropes and ducked

out of the way, and the *Andromeda* rose into the air in a steep climb. Roger would wait a few minutes until the whirlwind had moved on or dissipated before landing again. The passengers had gotten a thrill and a slightly longer flight than expected, so no goodwill was lost. It was the crew who trudged back into their lineup—dirty, sweating, and muttering curses at the weather, the airship, and everything in general.

The next landing was uneventful, and the crew breathed easier. Lexy checked her watch; the day was nearly over.

As the crew headed back to the bus she saw Cameron walking with Red and K.C., laughing. She quickened her pace to catch up and heard Cameron saying, "Come off it, guys, if she has a boyfriend back home, why would she want to fool around with me?"

Lexy listened as unobtrusively as possible, not sure she wanted to hear the conversation.

"Any woman would be crazy to turn you down, man—boyfriend or no," Red said. "If I had your looks and what you've got"—he and K.C. snickered suggestively—"I'd never be off my back."

K.C. protested, "Yeah, but, Red, I keep telling you, Cameron can have any kind of woman he chooses. Why would he want Lexy?"

Something constricted for a moment inside her as she waited for the reply.

"What's wrong with Lexy?" Cameron asked, his voice a little husky, the way it was in the bar that night of the fight.

K.C. shrugged. "Well, she's, you know—*Lexy.*"

"No, I don't know."

Red interceded. "What K.C. means is that he thinks you like women who are a little more like real women. Ones that are soft and feminine."

They were almost to the bus, and Lexy lagged back

a little farther, not wanting to hear what Cameron would say next but desperately needing to know. He had said just that morning that he liked women who were strong and firm, not soft. Had he been lying?

"Well, K.C., you're wrong. I like women who aren't fragile. I like women who can give a man a good tussle and who are fit and strong; that's sexy to me. You can have your simpering little girls—they're for kids anyway."

Cameron walked in to the bus, leaving K.C. and Red outside in the heat for a moment. Rather than approach, Lexy veered off toward the semitrailer for a drink from the water cooler. As she walked Mark and Kerry were soaking towels to wipe their faces and cool their necks. Patiently waiting for them to finish, she found them both staring at her.

"What's the joke?" Kerry asked.

"Joke?"

"Yeah, Lexy, you're grinning like a cat that just swallowed a tasty canary," Mark said.

"Oh, nothing," she replied.

Would tonight ever come? She checked her watch again.

After the next landing, Lexy sat in the bus, trying to read. Cameron seated himself right in front of her, leaning the seat back a little. His black hair curled against the blue vinyl seat upholstery as his head rested less than two feet away. She could see his arm on the armrest, the thick, dark hair on it covering the tanned muscles. His strong hand lay relaxed—the same hand that hours before was cradling her in the surging waters of the whirlpool, cupping her breast. . . .

She wondered if she had thought out loud, for

Cameron turned to look at her. He took off his mirrored sunglasses and smiled. "Warm, isn't it?"

"It is rather close in here," she managed to reply in a reasonable imitation of her real voice. "I can hardly wait for this day to be over."

Cameron smiled crookedly as if surprised. "I feel exactly the same way."

Was that the way it would be, she wondered—inane conversation that was anything but inane? To the crewmen around them, it meant nothing. They held the same kind of conversations with each other—idle, meaningless, to pass the time.

"Is there any good place to eat besides the hotel?" he asked.

Lexy shrugged, wondering if she was playing the game correctly. "I'm planning to have room service. I like being pampered."

Cameron's blue eyes twinkled as he peered over the back of his seat. "That sounds kind of good, come to think of it. Pampered privacy sounds like the perfect thing tonight."

Lexy swallowed a laugh and returned to trying to read her book.

Mercifully, Killigrew called the landing, and it was time to walk out again to catch the blimp.

The ride up in the hotel elevator seemed endless. Red, Sheldon, K.C., Deckard, Kerry, Cameron, and Lexy were crowded in, briefcases and all. It had always amused her that these rough, tough macho types carried briefcases just like the businessmen they disdained.

Kerry sniffed loudly. "Gawd, somebody needs a shower in here," he declared. Red jostled him and Kerry pushed back. "Whatsa matter, Red? You sweating?" Kerry draped his arm over Red's shoulder.

"Come on, guys. This is no place for horseplay," Lexy said, crushed into the corner behind Red.

"Aw, Lexy's grouchy," Deckard mumbled.

"Not grouchy," she said. "All I want is a shower and to get out of this uniform."

"Hey, Cam, why don't you give her a hand?" Red said, nudging Cameron in the ribs.

"Scrub her back," K.C. added.

Dryly, Lexy said, "I'm a big girl. I can scrub my own back." But the thought of it gave her a shiver of anticipation.

Finally the elevator doors opened on the fifth floor and they poured out like cattle out of a chute.

"That's what Cameron likes about you, Lexy," K.C. smirked. "You're a big girl."

"Can it, K.C.," Red snapped.

Cameron walked to his door as if he had not heard them. Lexy passed him, noting that only one room separated hers from his. She managed to get inside before the butterflies of excitement overwhelmed her.

Two hours later Lexy said to herself in the mirror, "This is stupid." She sat in her paisley robe, her hair brushed out and clean—showered, perfumed, and made up. The phone was a nasty beige toad sitting dumbly on the dresser under the mirror, into which she cursed at herself for acting like a schoolgirl. "I'm a big girl," she mocked. "And big girls can do anything they want."

She reached for the phone to call Cameron, since he had not called her. As she touched it it rang loudly. She jumped back as if bitten. She made a face at herself in the mirror, let it ring once again—so she wouldn't appear too eager—and snatched up the receiver.

"Hello," she said nonchalantly. It was Cameron, and she leaned on the corner of the dresser for support.

"Hi. Sorry I took so long to call. You want to eat together? You could have room service deliver to your room."

"What do you want?"

"Besides you?" There was laughter in his deep voice. "Steak and potatoes. Nothing fancy. And red wine. Gotta keep my strength up."

She was glad he couldn't see her goofy smile, her girlish giddiness. "How will you get here without being seen. I mean—"

"Unlock your balcony door."

"You can't—we're five stories up!"

"I checked. The balconies are only two feet from each other. Plenty of railing to hold on to. Where's your sense of romance?"

"You're crazy."

"I think so, but not for climbing balconies."

"Whose room is between us?"

"Deckard; he just went out with K.C. and Red to eat, so there won't be a problem being seen when I cross his balcony."

Lexy, the reader of romantic fiction, was appalled. "Climbing balconies and hiding from prying eyes— Cameron, are you sure about this?"

"Where's that madcap princess of passion who drove me wild in the whirlpool at six A.M.?"

Before she could answer he said, "Order the food, I'm starved," and hung up.

Lexy ordered the food, turned on the TV to a rerun of *Magnum, P.I.*, and waited. Moments later she heard a scratching at her balcony door and the glass slid aside. Cameron's lanky form dropped into the darkened room. Lexy switched off the TV and rose to meet him shyly.

Before she could stop herself, she said, "I hope you don't think I do this kind of thing all the time. Truth is, I've never had anybody climb across balconies to me or—."

"It's about time you started," he said, taking her into his arms. Cameron's mouth covered hers with a gentle kiss that seemed to extend all the way to somewhere behind her navel. Lexy kissed him back tentatively. He tasted of salt and the rich warmth that was him.

She pressed against him, a little weak in the knees. They parted and Cameron took a breath. "You're quite a woman. It's a good thing you hide it like you do."

"You bring it out in me. Actually, I'm rather surprised at myself."

"Why?"

"I'm new at being a hussy." She laughed and slid her arms around his neck to kiss him again. He was not so gentle this time, but devoured her mouth with his. His hands slid down to pull her hips against him. She felt him already hard against her.

"Can we go a little more slowly?" she asked breathlessly.

He nodded. "I'm sorry. I get carried away." He crossed to sit at the small table near the balcony door. "It's been a while—"

"This morning wasn't so long ago."

Cameron grinned sheepishly. "You're not sorry that it happened, are you?"

Lexy sat on the bed and tucked her feet under the edge of the robe. Suddenly she wished she were fully

117

dressed instead of wearing the long robe over what she had underneath.

"No, I'm not sorry. It was a physical release for both of us. I'm not a silly romantic; I recognize it for what it was."

"I hope that's not all you think it was."

She thought for a moment. "Cam, was it really more than that?"

Cameron rose and crossed to the bedside. "We can find out. . . ."

"I want you, Cameron Ramsay, like I can't remember wanting a man in a long time. But it frightens me too. What if we can't stand each other? What if we end up hating each other—both knowing all the intimate little details of each other as lovers?"

He towered over her, his blue eyes piercing her in the dim light. "You're afraid you're some kind of perverse trophy, aren't you?"

Lexy's chin jutted defiantly. "You can say you won't tell here and now, but what happens in the future?"

"You women are all alike," he said angrily.

"What's that supposed to mean?" she flared, standing up, hands on her hips.

"What about *my* reputation?" he demanded.

"Your reputation?"

"Yeah. How do I know you won't go in tomorrow and announce what happened? 'Cameron's a lousy lay: There's nothing to him—just rolls over and goes to sleep.' " He stepped closer to her, glaring down at her. "Yeah. How would that make me look? And on top of that, using me for a one-night stand—a fellow crewman. Where's your loyalty and sense of brotherhood? How could you do that?"

Lexy backed off, eyes wide and bewildered at the absurdity of his accusations.

Then a smile tugged at the full lips under his mustache, and his eyes glinted mischievously. "You could ruin me."

"I wouldn't—I couldn't—" she stammered. Then realization dawned that she was being had.

Cameron stepped closer. "I promised you this morning: You tell and I tell. We've got secrets on each other, old girl. So we'd better make the most of them." Once again his arms went around her, pulling her up against his chest. The blue chambray shirt that he wore matched his eyes and was open almost to the waist. She pressed her palms against his chest as their lips met again.

His hands tugged at the belt of her robe. It fell open to reveal what she wore underneath. His eyes widened, startled. Lexy blushed, suddenly feeling self-conscious.

She wore a black silk teddy camisole, tied with ribbons over desire-swollen breasts. It was tight, the flesh straining at the flimsy ribbons. Lace trimmed the high-cut legs and the straps. She packed it whenever she traveled, a frivolous dream that was fulfilled for the first time.

His voice was ragged as he took a breath. "You don't wear that under your uniform, do you?"

She laughed. "Of course not."

"Good. If I thought about you wearing something like that all day around me, I couldn't be responsible for my actions."

"What could you do on the field?" she asked playfully.

"This." With alarming swiftness Cameron lunged, pushing her back on the bed and covering her body with his before she could protest. His hands pinned her arms above her head and he stretched out over her, his long body hard against hers.

119

Her breasts jutted out, straining against the sheer black silk and lace. Hungrily his lips kissed her breasts through the delicate fabric.

Lexy whispered his name, writhing under him, not struggling to escape his imprisoning hands but struggling to feel him against her, rough and hard, so completely masculine. She wanted to put her arms around him, to run her fingers through his curly black hair as he nipped and nibbled at her breasts, but he refused to let her wrists escape. He paused to capture both in one hand, freeing his other to caress first her neck, then her other breast. He rubbed the calloused skin of his palm across the exquisitely sensitive silk-covered areola until she cried out breathlessly.

Then her wrists were loose and her hands were free to explore the broad expanse of his lean back as he lay atop her, then moved up clawing, stroking, tangling in the curly black hair of his head. She grabbed a fistful of hair, pulling his head back from the hollow between her breasts. He looked at her with languorous anticipation and she drew his mouth to hers, savagely kissing him and biting his lips, probing deeply with her tongue.

Someone knocked at the door and they heard the muffled voice say "Room service."

With a groan of agony, Cameron buried his face in her neck. "Just a moment," Lexy called, her voice unnaturally shrill from the shock of reality.

Cameron rolled off her and Lexy hurriedly repaired her robe and smoothed her tousled hair as Cameron bolted for the bathroom and closed the door.

A young bellman pushed a cart into the room—a table with a peach linen tablecloth, flowers, candles, a silver ice bucket, and plates with silver covers. Lexy smiled innocently at him as he looked around the room curiously.

"Dinner for two?" he asked with a puzzled grin.

"Yeah, I'm really hungry. Good night." She signed the tab, tipping him generously. Then she ushered him out before he could say anything more.

"You can come out now," Lexy called.

Cameron opened the bathroom door and peeked out. "I didn't want to take any chances when you opened the door. Besides, even bellmen talk, and a chance remark about you entertaining me might slip out."

She frowned. "You're an old hand at this kind of intrigue, aren't you?"

"New leaf, remember? Leave my past out of this or we'll simply end up fighting again."

Lexy was silent for a moment, then smiled. "Shall we dine?"

"I'd love to," Cameron said, sliding his arms around her again. "I'd like to start with you."

"I thought you were hungry."

He let her go and reached for a dish cover. "Come to think of it, you're right."

She shook her head, laughing. "I never know what to expect from you."

"Remember that, my dear."

Cameron insisted upon lighting the candles and switched off the lamp in the room. With soft music on the radio the evening became the perfect romantic dream.

They finished eating, toasted each other with the last of the wine, and peered into each other's eyes across the candlelit table.

"You really enjoy the romance, don't you?" Lexy asked finally. "Not many men do."

"Once in a while; don't think I'll put up with it

every time, though. Usually I'm a lot more direct, so don't be surprised."

"Oh," she said. "Soon it will be 'Got a minute?' "

"Cynical, aren't you?"

"I listen to you guys talk all day long. What do you expect?"

"It must sound pretty bad," he admitted.

Lexy stared into her wine, bloodred in the flickering candlelight. "Do you have any idea where this will lead, Cam?"

"To bed, I hope," he said with a roguish grin. "You're dressed for it."

"No, you know what I mean. This—whatever it is we're about to have." What could they call it? Affair? Encounter? Relationship?

He rose, moving around behind her chair. "What do you want me to say? 'Happily ever after'?"

Lexy tilted her head back to look up at the tall man who had come to mean so much to her in such a short time. "I don't expect 'happily ever afters,' Cam. 'Ever after' is simply made up of tomorrows, and tomorrows never come. We only have todays."

He pulled her into his arms. "I know there is a reason for your saying that, one that is probably hidden inside a hurt done to you. I want to know the story. I want to know all about you, and there will be plenty of time for learning. But right now I want to make love to you. I want to return some of the pleasure you gave me this morning."

"I enjoyed it too."

"Not like I did, I'll bet," Cameron said with a rueful grin. "Lady, you nearly killed me this morning in those few short minutes. I thought I was a goner for sure."

Lexy felt herself blushing. "But . . . you seemed to be so blasé about it afterward."

He kissed her nose. "You didn't see big, macho Cameron stagger back to his room and keel over like jelly for the rest of the morning. I nearly missed the bus, thanks to you."

A curious glow of satisfaction brought a smile to her lips. She caressed the soft hairs of his chest with her fingertips. She had never known a man to be so frank with her, so laughingly open and unembarrassed. Nor had she ever had a man tell her that he was so affected by her physically. It made her feel wicked and experienced. She trailed her fingernails down his chest and under his shirt to the waistline, where his jeans were snug against his flat belly.

"Come to bed and let me please you," Cameron said.

He took her hand and they crossed to the bed. He once more untied the belt of her robe and slid it off her shoulders, kissing her neck as he did so. She started to undo the ribbons of her camisole, but he took her hand away, pressing the fingers to his lips before he sat her down. "I'll do that," he offered.

He knelt before her, untying the ribbons that held the silk closed one at a time and planting kisses on the flesh of her breasts as he exposed them. With his teeth he teased the nipples into sharp rosy points, worrying them, exploring them until Alexandra leaned back on her elbows on the bed, her breath ragged. His lips moved downward, tasting her belly, his mustache tickling her navel. At the same time his hands slipped the straps of the camisole down until her breasts were fully exposed and he could toy with them even as he kissed her belly and the tops of her thighs.

She realized that he was tugging at the ribbons that held the bottom closed and sat back up to watch as his large hands, so gentle and sensual, parted the

123

fabric and pulled it away from the dark cleft between her white thighs. Curiously she felt no embarrassment, only that it was the most natural thing in the world that this man should be touching her in ways no one had for a long time—and even in some ways she'd never experienced before.

His moist tongue bathed her flesh, touching her with a magic glow that was first electric, then slowly sent such langor through her that she melted down across the bed. Her only thread of existence was her flesh and his touch, kissing, caressing, and driving her to a peak of feeling she had long ago forgotten.

She heard her own soft whimpering moan. "Cam, please—you'd better stop. . . ."

"No," he whispered. "Not yet." He refused to stop. Her hands clutched spasmodically at the bedspread; her hair was a tangle as her head tossed from side to side in the throes of ecstasy.

"Please," she moaned.

"Soon," he murmured, driving her still further with his mouth and his hands.

With her soft cry the wave began, spiraling her upward dizzily until she felt herself soaring and floating, then drifting lazily back down. At the precise moment she regained her ability to feel and think again, he was up beside her on the bed. He folded her into his arms, whispering softly, kissing her and holding her while the wild beating of her heart calmed and she caught her breath.

Softly his lips brushed hers and she tasted her own muskiness. She snuggled closer to his chest, wishing she could nestle deeply in his arms and stay there.

After a few more moments he rolled away to slip off his shirt and jeans. He stood for a few seconds, towering over the edge of the bed, lean, lanky and well muscled. Like a panther, he crawled across the bed to her, naked and erect, and lay down across her body, covering it with his. He moved against her, his hardness hot against her thigh.

"What do you want?" he whispered. "Tell me what you want."

She heard herself telling him—talking in ways she had always wanted to but never had with the men she had known. Nothing seemed to be hidden between them. She knew that no matter what she said, he understood.

The darkness became a dizzying tumult of passionate caresses and savage but tender twisting and thrusting, murmurs of longing and desire, moans of release and pleasure.

Then he faced her once again, looking into her eyes as he met his own needs. Lexy watched his face, letting her own passion and need ebb for a moment while she reveled in his.

Watching him, she felt it begin for her again, and she whispered his name in the same moment that he groaned softly with her, shuddering, exploding inside her as she met it with her own storm.

They collapsed, entwined. With a monumental effort he turned his head from where it was buried in the pillow and peered at her with one eye open. "Forgive me, my dear."

"Why?" she whispered. "You're wonderful."

He smiled impishly. "Except I'm one of those wretches who rolls over and falls asleep."

With that, he kissed her and rolled over. Wearily he pulled her into his arms and with a distracted smile at her murmured, "Did you set your alarm?"

Before she could answer she heard a soft snore. *Wretch*, she thought with a smile. She glanced at her alarm clock. She had set it for four A.M., just before dawn.

A moment later Lexy was asleep beside him.

The alarm dinged loudly in the dark room and she awoke groggily in the darkness, confused for a moment. She sat up, startled at the sound of movement in the room.

Cameron, sitting on the bed, shushed her. "It's only me." He kissed her softly on her sleep-swollen lips. Lexy slid her arms around him. He was already dressed. She rested her cheek on his shoulder and he smoothed her tangled hair back.

"I'm taking my chances in the corridor rather than cross Deckard's balcony."

She nodded. "Good. Deck is liable to shoot first and never get around to the questions."

Cameron kissed her again. "You're terrific." He rose and moved to the door.

"Cam?" Lexy pulled her knees up to her breasts under the covers.

He paused. "Hmmm?"

"Thanks."

"My pleasure, ma'am." He tipped an imaginary hat with a rakish smile. He peeked into the corridor, winked at her, then slipped away.

CHAPTER TEN

"Airship!" Killigrew called.

Lexy heaved herself stiffly out of her seat in the bus and began the long walk out across the hot, dusty field. Today was not much different than yesterday. Except today she was sore in places she couldn't complain about to anyone except Cameron. When she was able to mention it in a private moment in the truck early in the day, he merely grinned wickedly.

"Serves you right, wanton hussy."

Lexy had to conceal the smile of satisfaction Cameron's remark brought to her lips. As they walked out to the lineup for one of the last flights of the day, she shook her head as if it might make what had happened the night before more real since it was still dreamlike, a fantasy.

Yet, it had been true. A man had come over the balconies to a candlelit dinner and seduction. At dawn he had disappeared down the corridor.

Lexy watched Cameron's broad back ahead of her, the white uniform shirt stretched tightly across his shoulders, and she thought of how the skin underneath it had felt—warm and moist from the sweat of their passion. The long legs in navy blue uniform pants had been bristly against her own smooth ones in the cool darkness of her room. . . .

"Lexy?" came Mark's voice. "Are you okay?"

"Hmm?" she said. "Yes, why?"

"You had a glazed look on your face, and you're kind of pale. You're sure the heat's not getting to you?"

"No," she murmured. "Not the heat."

Mark and Deckard looked at each other and shrugged. Deckard grumbled, "I think she watched the late show last night; sounded like it when I got in. She needs to get more sleep instead of watching old movies."

Lexy nodded numbly. "Sorry, Deck, I'll keep the sound down from now on."

When she returned to the hotel after the day was finished, she found a telephone message she had been expecting: *Meet me at the airport, 8:00. Don't tell Red.* It was from Nancy Riley. She and Lexy had worked out the surprise weeks ago to celebrate the Rileys' fifteenth wedding anniversary.

After a quick change and shower Lexy headed down to sign out the company van. As she passed the coffee shop she saw Red and Cameron having dinner. Her heart lurched a little upon seeing Cameron, but she casually waved. They motioned her to join them, but she shook her head. She didn't go in, since it would mean an explanation, so she simply tapped her watch as if late for something and hurried out.

Nancy was waiting at the airport, her face brimming with excitement. She had already claimed her luggage and stood on the curbside in the heat, awaiting the sight of the Vulcan company van. Nancy was short and plump, but had a good figure for a woman who had had four children and whose husband's favorite food was pasta. Her hair was stylishly cut, and she wore a tailored linen pantsuit that showed off her full figure to advantage. Lexy liked Nancy for her sense of humor and her spirit, and for the determination with which she worked at her marriage to Red, who was a handful at his best.

Nancy and Lexy chatted about the kids and the other wives who were not traveling, and Lexy filled Nancy in about the ones who were. Lexy ignored any "juicy" gossip, keeping only to the generalized news —the standard scuttlebutt.

And oh, yes, the new fellow Cameron Ramsay was very nice, Lexy admitted, although they did have a slight personality conflict.

Nancy's eyes lit up at once. "Trouble with Cam already?"

"We can't seem to get along," Lexy lied, disliking it as she said it.

"But Cam is a sweet, charming man. I've had a crush on him for years."

Lexy smiled. "Does Red know?"

Nancy laughed. "Red tells me that if he could take over Cam's body for one day, I'd be the happiest woman on the face of this earth."

You ain't just whistlin' "Dixie," Lexy thought as she pulled the van into the hotel parking lot.

Lexy headed into the lobby to make sure the coast was clear, while a bellman helped Nancy with the luggage.

Meanwhile, Red and Cameron had finished dinner and gone upstairs to their rooms. As they came out of the elevator they saw a familiar woman standing outside Red's door, knocking insistently.

Red looked at Cameron sheepishly. "It's that broad, Carol. She was bugging me in the bar the other night."

"Red, you don't have to explain to me," Cameron said. "I've known you for years."

"Hey, I nearly lost Nancy two years ago over some peroxide blonde whose name I didn't even know. I

129

don't take any chances; I'm not interested. Guilt alone would get me. Tomorrow's my anniversary. Nancy will probably phone. That's why I want to stay in my room tonight."

The redhead, Carol, turned at the sound of voices, "Hi, honey," she called. "I was looking for you."

"Carol, I told you—"

As they met her in the corridor she slipped her arm through Red's. His florid color deepened. "Cam—"

Cameron held up his hands. "Red, it's up to you. I don't get involved in these things; I always get in trouble."

Cameron walked on. Carol said in a kittenish voice, "Let's go in your room and talk. I told you I'd be glad to *negotiate* about a ride on the blimp."

As Red opened his door Cameron heard him tell her once again, "I can't get you a ride. I told you that in the bar. . . ."

He should never have let her in, Cameron thought to himself. His room was next to Red's with a connecting door that was locked on both sides. Briefly, Cameron considered knocking on it to try to help Red out, but backed off, knowing he always got into trouble trying to bail somebody else out.

To avoid the temptation, Cameron took the elevator to the lobby to pick up an evening paper at the newsstand. It was as he rounded the corner to the elevator that he saw Lexy. His eager smile faded as he saw who was standing with her: Nancy Riley.

Before they saw him, Cameron walked nonchalantly back around the corner, and as soon as he was out of sight he bolted for the stairs at a full run. He knew there would be trouble and he was getting himself into it.

By the time he pounded up to the fifth floor, his knee was paining him and he was out of breath. He heard the ding of the elevator door and women's voices, and dashed down the hallway to his room.

He managed to throw himself through the door before they came around the corner. Cameron pounded wildly on the connecting door. Inside, Red fumbled with the lock while Carol chattered in the background.

Red looked relieved as he opened the door. Cameron, who was out of breath from the wild dash up the steps, could only gasp *"Nancy!"* and lunge into Red's room, grab Carol by the arm, snatch her handbag, and drag her past Red.

Carol's protests rose to a shriek and Cameron clapped his hand over her mouth. There was a knock on Red's outer door. Cameron gasped *"Nancy!"* again. Realization dawned and a look of horror spread over Red's face. He slammed the connecting door and slid the bolt home, leaving Cameron with Carol, who was now foot-stamping, shin-kicking mad.

Cameron tried to shush her to try to explain, but she wrenched herself out of his clutches, marched to the door, and jerked it open before he could stop her.

Carol stomped out, swearing like an experienced mule skinner, shoving past the two women and the bellman standing in the corridor. Cameron froze as he saw Lexy—and Lexy saw Carol!

With a groan Cameron slumped against the door-jamb.

The expression on Lexy's face said it all. It didn't help when Nancy added, "Well, hello, Cam. Up to your old tricks, I see. Too bad your taste in women hasn't improved."

As Carol stomped past, Red stood in the open door, slack-jawed. "Nancy," he croaked. She rushed

131

into his arms, oblivious to the reason for his shock—that of narrow escape—and Red enfolded her in a bear hug.

The bellman shouldered past them with the luggage, and Lexy stiffly handed Red the bouquet of flowers that Nancy had insisted upon buying at the last minute in the lobby. "Happy Anniversary," she whispered woodenly.

Cameron stood in his doorway, a miserable expression on his face. Lexy stared at him for a moment, her face a mask. Then she turned on her heel and walked to her own room, slamming the door.

When the bellman came out, he glanced at the tall man in the next doorway beating his head against the jamb, mumbling, "No, *no, no*—I knew it, *I knew it.*"

Lexy made it to her bed before the angry tears cascaded down her cheeks. She slammed her fist into the pillow, wishing it were Cameron. She had believed him—*believed* him—when he had said all those wonderful things to her, all those things about what kind of woman she was. Worse, she had believed him when he said he had turned over a new leaf, that he was no longer interested in one-night stands. Then she had let him sweet-talk her like a fifteen-year-old virgin—right into her own bed.

How could I? she demanded. *How could I let myself fall for the line of a womanizing sexual athlete like Cameron Ramsay?*

The phone rang.

Lexy let it ring twice more while she wiped away the hot tears. "Hello?" she said quietly, trying to hide the sound of crying in her voice.

"Lexy—" It was Cameron.

"Cameron, don't bother. You've had your little fling—accomplished what you set out to."

"Can't I at least see you and try to explain?"

"There is nothing to explain." She hoped he could not hear the catch in her voice.

He was silent for a moment. "All right. If that's the way you want it."

"I can only hope you'll keep your word about—"

His voice was hard, angry. "You'll have to wait and see, won't you?"

The implication was like a slap in the face. Horrified, she sat down at the desk, her knees unable to hold her up. She could already hear the jeering and the laughter from the crew, the snide remarks and asides, the slaps on the back he would get.

"Good-bye," she said softly, and hung up.

CHAPTER ELEVEN

The last day in Pasco was the most miserable of all. It was hot and virtually windless. The landings were hard. The dust boiled up with every step. Tempers were short, and the smallest things brought flashes of anger and harsh words, even among best friends.

For the previous three days Lexy had once more withdrawn, reading between landings, carrying out her duties with as little conversation as possible. She felt that if she made herself inconspicuous, perhaps Cameron would not be provoked into spilling their secret to the rest of the crew.

Invariably it was at the worst of times like these that clients and VIPs seemed to insist upon meeting the crew, and for the second time that day the crew was trotted out by PR to put their collective best foot forward.

This time it was three trucking-company owners, from somewhere near the Idaho border, who had come to Pasco just to take a ride on the blimp, courtesy of the Vulcan district office.

Sammy Florsheim passed out Vulcan blimp souvenir caps and introduced the three trucking executives to "our boys." Lexy hung back a little, trying to stay away from Cameron, but somehow ended up beside him.

One of the VIPs, a fat, florid man in a Hawaiian

shirt, shook Cameron's hand, then nudged his buddies. "Got a woman too. What's she do?" he said, as if Lexy were not even present.

"Same thing as the other crewmen, sir," Lexy replied. She tried to keep the irritated edge from her tone.

The three seemed amused that she could speak for herself, and laughed tolerantly. As they walked on to look over the tractor trailer, she heard the fat one tell the other two, "Looks to me like she could do a lot more than the other crewmen."

Several of the crew heard it, including Cameron. His mouth compressed into a grim line, but it was Kerry who took two steps after them. Cameron caught his arm.

"It's not worth it, Kerry," he said.

Kerry stared at him, then at Lexy.

She turned away, her throat tight. "He's right, Kerry. Leave it."

Cameron watched her walk away, his face grim. Kerry was still staring at him. "All week long you been on her case, Cam. Why?"

"We don't work well together," was all he said.

Lexy found her seat on the bus and stared out the window. She wondered how long she would hate him, how long before her hate was reduced to numbness. Weeks? Months? Why didn't he tell them and get it over with? Was he holding out for the most effective moment?

After the last flight when the ship was secured to the mooring mast and the passengers were gone, the worst happened. A whirlwind appeared almost like a small explosion around the truck, swirling in a column of dust a hundred feet high in the distance between the truck and the ship.

135

"Whirlwind!" someone screamed. For a moment everyone was frozen. It was Cameron who lunged at the handrail to flip on the control switch to the pressure box. The blower kicked in, raising the internal pressure of the blimp just as the ship was lifted into the air, twisting on the nose mooring.

Caught making an instrument check in the cockpit, Mark was a white-faced wraith, bracing himself against the instrument panel to keep from falling forward as the *Andromeda*'s tail was sucked into the air while the whirlwind spun past in a tornado cloud. The crew scattered to the outer perimeters of the mast as the ship rose to stand on her nose, swinging wildly in the winds of the dust devil. Ballast bags tumbled free from the ballast compartment to fall like twenty-five-pound bombs. Crewmen dodged them while trying to stay close enough to the ship to help when she would come plummeting down.

Then the whirlwind was gone, spinning wildly toward the hangars to rip and tear at the small planes moored there. Left without the suction of the wind, the *Andromeda* hovered for a moment, balanced on her nose, then dropped back to earth as if shoved by a giant invisible hand from above.

Lexy leaped across the mast box and ran to the ship with most of the other crewmen. As one, they tried to get under the gondola and push and pull it sideways to lessen the direct impact of the weight of the falling blimp on the landing gear. But the *Andromeda* hit hard; her landing gear groaned, shock absorbers spread to their maximum. The belly valves belched with the impact. The control box hanging on the railing around the bottom of the gondola broke loose, trailing by its cables.

The crew was able to diminish the impact slightly, but the force again bounced the ship off the landing gear and up into the air. A few crewmen held on, hoping their extra weight would settle the airship back to the ground.

Lexy was among those hanging on as the ship rose again into the air twenty feet. She shut her eyes, hanging too high to let go, praying it would go no higher. She opened them long enough to see who else had hung on and saw George and Deckard. *But Deck hates heights,* she thought. Then they were dropping slowly again as the ship settled in.

Within five feet of the ground Lexy let go and twisted away from the ship, while on the other side, Deckard and George did the same. The other crewmen rushed in to steady the ship, which finally shifted, bounced a few feet again, and was once more stable, bobbing lazily as if nothing had happened.

Mark catapulted out of the cockpit and down the ladder, white-faced. He grinned shakily as he hit the ground. Someone asked, "How was the flight?"

Regaining his composure, ever the mechanic, Mark crawled under the gondola to check the landing gear. The rest of the crew fanned out to check for surface damage. "I'll get your tools," Kerry called to Mark, heading for the truck.

"Need some help?" Lexy asked.

A hand fell on her arm and she turned to face Cameron, who was grim-faced and angry. "What the hell was that stunt?"

"Stunt?"

"Hanging on like that. You could have been hurt."

Lexy stepped back, jaw set, fists clenched. "I don't hear you yelling at Deck or George."

"They're not—" Cameron began.

"What?"

Cameron pivoted on his heel and strode away.

The terror of the moment was gone now, and Lexy

found herself shaking slightly, but she was unsure if it was due to the near accident or Cameron's anger.

In the distance another, smaller dust devil played around the corner of the hangar, and Lexy cursed the eastern desert of Washington.

Early the next morning at the mast site, Art Guthrie made the announcement about the change in schedule. "It will mean an extra long day, but we're heading back down the Columbia River to Portland and skipping Yakima. I've checked with the home office and they've okayed it: The weather conditions are a little too hazardous this time of year to stay. It's not worth the airship to butter up a few customers here."

A cheer went up from the crew, and he grinned a self-satisfied smile. "I hope you guys remember this when you buy the beer."

"How long in Portland?" Killigrew asked.

"A week. I want the landing gear changed completely, and a full inspection. I know the mechanics didn't find anything wrong on the initial examination, but I don't want to take any chances."

So instead of a short drive to Yakima, it would be a long haul to Portland; but no one on the crew was unhappy with the prospect of temperate days and mild nights. It was a much more cheerful crew that launched the *Andromeda* into the bright blue desert sky.

The sight of the Columbia River Gorge at The Dalles was a joy to the crew. Even the wind-ruffled water that told them the *Andromeda* was fighting a headwind was not dismaying—not after Pasco.

Guthrie was in radio contact with pilots Roger and

Terry in the airship and announced, "We'll refuel before lunch."

The convoy of Vulcan vehicles turned off the main highway, crossing the bridge over the locks to head toward the little airport outside of The Dalles.

Lexy was driving the bus and geared down to follow at the semi's slow pace. Cameron was driving the company van between the two larger vehicles, and she could see his unsmiling face and mirrored sunglasses in his rearview mirror. She made a face, hoping he would see her yet hoping he wouldn't, since it was so childish.

The tension between them was a palpable thing now, and most of the crew figured it was out-and-out hatred born of their personality differences. The only one about whom Lexy wondered was Killigrew. He always seemed to be watching them both with wise old eyes. In an attempt to throw him off, she forced unflagging good humor and cheer on the bus, chattering merrily away on the long trip down from Pasco.

But Killigrew was not fooled as he saw her pull the face at Cameron ahead in the van. "You start something you can't finish?" he asked finally, leaning forward so no one else could hear. Lexy wheeled the bus around the last turn into the tiny airport.

"Have you heard some juicy gossip I don't know about?" she asked after a moment, trying to sound nonchalant.

"Is there some to hear?"

Lexy pulled the parking brake and turned to peer indignantly at Killigrew. "Brant, if you're baiting me for information, it won't work."

"You mean you got information you don't want let out?"

She bit back her temper as Killigrew added, "Just thought I'd ask. . . ."

She opened the door and bounded down the steps into the cool afternoon wind, such a change from the oppressive heat of the desert hours before. The wind was blowing about thirty miles an hour, and worried mutters ran among the crew. Refueling would not be easy.

Lexy headed to the truck to help pull out the fuel cans they would carry out to the ship when it landed. It would be a fast-moving, harrowing operation in the high winds.

There was an edge to the crew that the danger brought out. They laughed and joked about the grimmer aspects of the situation, taking mock bets on how long the ship might float in the Columbia River if she ran out of fuel; or which captain had to go down with her, Roger or Terry; or would Guthrie, being in charge, be required by protocol to swim out to sink with his ship? Lexy found their humor too grim, but she knew it was only a way of releasing the tension and fear of it actually happening.

Lining up for the landing, Lexy found herself with K.C., Kerry, and Deckard. They all stood anxious, silent, as the ship approached with engines howling at full power against the wind. Roger was fighting every inch of the way as he neared the ground. The crew ran out to meet the ship and take the ropes, and the battle was on.

At first Lexy's line had to outrun the ship as it lurched wide to their side; then they were snapped around as it pitched the other way. The linemen fought it to a standstill. Red climbed into the aft compartment to pump, and the process of carrying out and handing off the red five-gallon cans began.

The part that frightened her was that, because of

the wind, both engines had to keep going while the full fuel cans were being handed up three feet in front of the spinning propeller. One slip and a fuel can hitting the prop would explode, or a man stumbling and falling would mean instant death.

Lexy watched George and Cameron—selected for their strength and size—carry the thirty-five-pound cans of fuel two at a time to the ship. They had to run while carrying them, moving with the pitching gondola, then ducking in to hand the cans up to Red. It took about a minute per can to pump up the five gallons, each minute dragging longer and longer.

Roger throttled up the engines a little, fighting for all the stability and control he could as Killigrew threw the linemen signals to keep the ship steady.

For a moment the wind seemed to die a little; then a gust pitched the ship wildly. Cameron was in the process of handing up a second fuel can as the gondola shifted his way. Off balance with the fuel can high over his head, Lexy saw him totter back a step. Red lunged to grab the handle of the fuel can, pulling it safely inside. Cameron grabbed the handrail as he fell sideways, and Lexy heard herself cry out.

The airship rolled back, righting herself. Cameron let himself be dragged a few feet, then regained his balance and ran for more fuel cans.

Killigrew threw a signal to the other line as the ship lurched again and Lexy and her line ran to keep the slack out, then were whipped back as they tried to stop the seesawing. The line burned along her forearm as it snapped tight. They fought the blimp in a wild waltz that seemed like it would never end.

Finally, arms aching and hands stiff, they watched the *Andromeda* shoot upward into the afternoon sky.

All twenty fuel cans were empty, lying like casualties at the side of the runway. Wearily the crew moved to collect them. They laughed and kidded among themselves, grateful that the dangerous refueling was over and the ship was safely on its last leg to more peaceful skies.

Walking along the taxiway toward the vehicles, Lexy noticed Cameron ahead of her, slower than the rest and trying hard to hide his limp. K.C. caught up to him and slapped him on the shoulder.

"Thought you were a goner for sure, Cam."

"So did I," Cameron said quietly.

K.C. shot Lexy a sly look. "So did Lexy: She was making all kinds of weird noises."

Lexy felt her face flame with embarrassment. She climbed back onto the bus, her head held high with dignity she was far from feeling. George was already in the driver's seat. Lexy reached into the overhead and pulled down the first-aid kit to get cream and a gauze pad for the welt on her arm. Beside it was a smaller box. She deliberated, then reached into it and extracted a blue plastic package that was a chemical cold pack.

Cameron brushed past her in the aisle, making his way to a seat toward the back. Lexy walked to the back of the bus with her first-aid supplies. As she passed his seat she dropped the cold pack beside him. He glanced up at her and wordlessly took the cold pack to apply to his knee.

Lexy sat at the desk in the rear to concentrate on fixing the rope burn on her arm. While she patched that, she concentrated on patching up her emotional turmoil as well.

She hated him for his lying and deceiving, but she could not avoid a fact: No matter what, she cared about him. In spite of her denials, her promises to herself, her pride and her dignity, she was in love with the worst possible man in the world.

142

"Damn," she hissed as she put the gauze pad in place.

"Hurt?" came Cameron's voice from behind her.

"Yeah," Lexy said. "Hurts a lot."

"Give it a little time."

"I think a lot of time," Lexy replied. She looked up at him then, to see that he was not wearing his sunglasses. She could see his blue eyes, narrow from the pain in his knee—and perhaps something else.

"Thanks for the cold pack."

"If it doesn't work on your knee, you could try it somewhere else." The words were out of her mouth before she could stop them.

Cameron smirked as if glad for the opening. "Come to think of it, I don't really need this. Just touch my knee and it'll be cold enough."

Lexy tensed, getting slowly to her feet, furious. "You need not worry about me ever touching anything of yours."

She pushed past him, heading for the front of the bus. Around them a few of the other crewmen had heard the exchange and studiously found other things to concentrate on as Lexy passed them to sit as far away from Cameron as she could possibly get.

CHAPTER TWELVE

Lexy sat once more in the Cave Bar, sipping white wine and staring out into the shadowy Columbia River. Sylvia was across the bar, pouring drinks for a couple of three-piece-suit types drinking beer and discussing a heavy-machinery sale. Besides them, they were alone in the bar.

Fortunately, most of the crew was still out at Portland International Airport at the blimp mooring site, on maintenance. Lexy had already worked a thirteen-hour day, having stood first watch from four A.M. until launch time. Her accumulated hours made her ineligible to join the maintenance party on overtime.

She was far from happy for a couple of reasons. The last couple of days since their arrival, she had been depressed and had stayed away from everyone —in particular Cameron. Since she had morning watch, and he had drawn the evening watch during the maintenance party, she wouldn't have to see him.

It was depression that drove her to the Cave Bar to seek answers in white wine and conversation with Sylvia. As usual, the motherly bartender was more than happy to talk between serving drinks.

Sylvia rang up the businessmen's beers on their tab, then turned back to stand in front of Alexandra. To justify their conversation, Sylvia wiped the glasses she had just removed from the dishwasher under the bar.

"Okay. So you've found a guy with that certain spark you were talking about last time. You had a little fling—"

"Sylvia, I didn't say that."

"You don't have to. I can tell. You look different since the last time you were in here. I can't put my finger on it, but it's different." Sylvia smiled gently. "Your secret is safe with me."

Lexy stared at her wineglass, embarrassed. "I'm afraid to go around him, now. I'm worried that anything I might say or do might set him off and he'll tell the rest of the crew."

"But he hasn't said anything yet?"

"No," Lexy said.

With a confident tone Sylvia said, "Then he won't. If he didn't do it right away, he won't do it at all."

Sylvia glanced across at the businessmen, who were still deep in conversation. Satisfied that she wasn't needed, she continued, "Why don't you just talk to him?"

"I can't." Lexy shook her head, taking another sip. "I wouldn't give him the satisfaction, particularly if he really lied to me and told me all those things just to—"

"What things?" Sylvia leaned over conspiratorially.

"Just . . . things," Lexy said. Some of them came back—the whispered endearments, sometimes muffled by flesh or slurred by sleepiness. She drove the thoughts from her mind.

Realizing that Lexy would not clarify, Sylvia returned to wiping glasses. "Did he tell you he loved you?"

"No." Of all the wonderful things he had said, that was not one of them. Tears stung her eyes.

"And neither of you made any promises, did you?"

"No." After all, it had been Lexy herself who told him she did not believe in "happily ever after"s.

Sylvia was silent for a moment, as if contemplating something serious. Finally she said, "You really want an opinion, or do you want me to tell you what you'd like to hear?"

Lexy smiled at her directness. "The opinion, Sylvia. I need a friend right now, not a bartender."

"Okay." She laid down the towel and leaned over again, lowering her voice. "Let it go. If it was a fling —whether you were taken for a ride by him or not— it's apparently over. It didn't work. You can't or won't try to patch it up, so you have to let it go."

"But he—"

"Don't try to second-guess the man. You don't know him well enough," Sylvia continued quietly. "And stop the 'But he—'s, stop thinking about him, stop fighting the battles over and over in your mind."

Lexy fought the tears that burned in her eyes. "You're right, Sylvia."

"Do you love him?"

"I guess I don't even have the dignity of saying no. I fell for him like a rock."

"Work with him as if nothing ever happened. Stay away from him as much as you can. But never let it show again. You'll live. It won't be easy, but *you'll live.*"

Lexy smiled and drank down her wine. "Thanks, Sylvia. I don't feel quite so stupid."

"Remember, love isn't an exact science. It makes fools out of everybody." Sylvia noticed that the businessmen were ready for more beers. "Hey, who ever said you have to be Wonder Woman, anyway? Why not take some time off?"

Lexy signed her tab and said, "You're terrific, Sylvia. Thanks."

Lexy headed for the house phone to call Killigrew. A couple of days off was exactly what she needed.

Lexy rented a car and drove west out of Portland. She intended to spend at least two days of her three-day vacation on the rocky, picturesque Oregon coastline, taking some photos and sightseeing. She headed for Tillamook, through forests so green, they seemed almost unreal, eerily shrouded in predawn fog and shadow like an unending fantasy painting.

The farther she drove from Portland, the happier she was. No, she corrected herself, the farther from Cameron Ramsay she was . . . but she corrected herself again. She knew better. The farther she drove from Alexandra Prince, Airship Crewman, the better off she was. She had to take a step outside of herself, to escape for a while. She had to relax and be a woman in jeans, with her hair unbraided and her time unfettered.

It was a little after dawn as she turned off the highway toward the gigantic wooden buildings with the curved roofs that loomed in the early-morning mists. The hangars had originally been built during World War Two to house the naval blimps used for aerial patrols along the coast. As some of the largest wooden structures in the country, they had been preserved as historical landmarks, even though they were now privately owned.

The Louisiana Pacific Lumber Company owned them, operating a sawmill in one, the last Lexy had heard. The other one, which she now paralleled as she drove toward the entrance to the property, was her objective. In the unused portion an aerostat—an experimental airship meant for heavy-lift cargo transport—was under construction by a private Canadian-backed firm.

Lexy wanted to photograph it for her airship album, and it certainly seemed like a good adventure for a day off. She rolled down her window to get a better look, through the early morning fog, at the half-open entrance, where an immense ghostly shape hovered in the barely lit interior.

The unmistakable sound of a pressure blower whined across the silent grounds. She would have known there was an airship there somewhere just by that sound alone. She parked her car in the shelter of a small wooden outbuilding and put on her denim jacket. Then she pulled out her camera and checked the settings, scanning the area for any signs of watchmen or security guards. None were apparent, so she started toward the giant hangar.

Moments later she peeked around the edge of the hangar door. She snapped a shot of the hangar itself from the ground to the top, just to remind herself of its size—more than two hundred feet from ground to roof. The doors had to be at least 150 feet tall. She stepped across the steel railroad track that was the guide for the immense sliding door, now half open.

The aerostat was moored by ground lines in the shelter of the hangar, a giant, white ovoid with slender fins set in a Y configuration—three fins instead of four, which the *Andromeda* had. It was alien-looking, more like some kind of spaceship than an airship.

Rumor throughout the airship circles was that it was so radically different that it might not even fly. Lexy hoped it would, for like the *Andromeda*, it seemed to possess a life of its own, sitting alone in the tremendous hangar. It deserved the open sky and

148

freedom. Though secured by cables, the lighter-than-air craft shifted and bobbed slightly in the almost still air of the chilly hangar.

A sound from somewhere farther inside sent Lexy scuttling into the shadows cast by the framework of the giant hangar doors. Dwarfed by the structure, Lexy crouched in the darkness and hid. Her heart was pounding from the excitement of seeing this strange airship and from the fear of getting caught trespassing.

The working of her camera seemed deafening in the silence of the hangar. Soft creaking came from the cables of the aerostat, and in the distance an owl called out eerily, echoing and reechoing. A noise became distinguishable: footsteps on the concrete floor. Lexy snapped some more photos, knowing that soon she would have to sneak back out by the red-lettered NO TRESPASSING sign she had passed on the way in.

Silhouetted against a light from a small doorway deep inside the quarter-mile-long building, Lexy could see a security guard walking slowly toward her end. She slipped out of her hiding place and ducked toward the dark corner of the hangar fifty feet away. She wanted to get around the end of the aerostat for a couple of shots of the odd little control gondola that was suspended on a yoke-shaped keel amidships. Just a couple shots of that and she could slip back out before the security guard got all the way down there.

Sheltered behind some packing crates, she watched the guard cross to the far side to check some doors. He disappeared behind a truck dwarfed by the crane parked beside it. Once he disappeared, Lexy decided to make one further foray—to the other side of the hangar to catch a few shots of the fins and empennage of the tail. Caught up in the moment, she felt like a spy infiltrating an enemy installation. She ran on her toes, her camera cradled against her breasts, and ducked into the shelter of a stack of wooden cable reels.

Then, in a moment of dizzying terror, an arm snaked around her waist, yanking her to her feet. A large, salty hand clapped over her mouth and her head was snapped back against a leather jacket. Lexy bucked wildly, panicked at her imprisonment.

She clutched at the hand suffocating her, but was dragged, kicking, farther into the recesses of the dark hangar, toward a corner with wooden crates and machinery. He shook her, muttering *"Quiet!"* in a harsh whisper.

She froze, aching with wide-eyed shock. *It couldn't be*—

She twisted in his arms to stare up into those damned blue eyes. Cameron Ramsay glared back. "What the hell are you doing here?" he demanded in a whisper.

Lexy pushed against him with all her considerable strength, but he held her fast with his. "I might ask you the same thing," she snapped.

"Shut up—the guard's heading this way. Did you get some pictures?"

Lexy nodded. She could feel his camera crushed between their bodies, and her own camera biting into her ribs and breasts.

"Good," Cameron said, but his arms did not relinquish their hold. Instead he bent down to cover her lips with his in a bruising kiss that raised the pounding of the blood in Lexy's ears to a thunder. Suddenly nothing mattered around them. Her arms slid around him and her lips softened under his until she thought she would melt into him.

They parted finally, after he had kissed her twice more—softly, quickly, as if stealing from her.

Then they were back to reality—in the hangar, trespassers in the early morning, with another company's airship hovering over their heads and a security guard walking slowly their way.

Cameron took her hand. "Let's go," he said, and they ran for the open door and the morning sunshine beyond.

The little café they found in Tillamook looked like something out of the fifties, with a dark linoleum floor and a screen door that banged behind them as they walked in. Some of the locals glanced up, then went back to their morning coffee and homemade sweet rolls. The young couple—she in denim, he in battered leather jacket and cowboy boots—were obviously strangers traveling through.

Lexy picked a table and slid into the beat-up aluminum-frame chair with the red vinyl seat patched with tape. Cameron folded his long legs under the yellowed Formica table and opened the cracked leatherette folder with *Menu* written in faded gold script. The typed menu inside was simple and inexpensive.

Lexy scanned her menu and, for wont of anything else, said, "Quite a change from the Modoc coffee shop."

"I'll bet the food's better," Cameron said, eyes still glued to the menu.

Their rental cars were parked across the street. They had driven in from the Louisiana Pacific hangars outside of town, and Lexy had picked this little restaurant on an impulse—probably the only one open at seven A.M. in the quiet little Oregon town. She had no time to refuse Cameron's hasty invitation to have breakfast once they cleared the hangar, with

151

the security guard shouting after them. Lexy had run toward her car and had driven off with her heart in her throat.

She knew it was not the prospect of getting caught trespassing: The worst that would have happened was that the guard would have called the sheriff, with a minor fine the end result. Such escapades were old hat for her in college days. This was a fear of the unknown, of losing something she could barely define, but something that meant more to her than she could admit.

"I didn't know you planned to take time off," Cameron said, toying with his silverware as if he had nothing to direct his attention at but that. "Funny how we thought of doing the same thing at the same time."

"I called Killigrew last night. I had to get away," she replied.

"From what?" She knew he knew the answer before she said it.

"You."

"Do you hate me that much?"

The waitress appeared with the pot of coffee to save them both from the answer that was already visible on Lexy's face. The waitress was young, tired-looking, with a calico blouse and jeans under her freshly starched apron. Her smile slipped a little as she looked from Lexy to Cameron. The unhappiness was like an invisible cloud between them.

Lexy mumbled her order of a poached egg, toast, and tea. Cameron ordered and the waitress escaped.

With deliberate care he replaced the menu between the glass sugar container and the battered chrome napkin box.

"I thought you were a pancake-and-egg–eater. What's this old-lady's breakfast?"

She shrugged. "Not hungry, I guess."

"This is a little less elegant than I had hoped for our first breakfast together," Cameron said, looking around the café.

"Perhaps it's not working out because I'm not familiar with the role I'm supposed to be playing."

"Role?" His expression was wary, guarded, as if he **knew a** storm was brewing.

"*Mistress,* I guess, would be a polite term. I've heard a lot of the less polite ones over the years from the rest of the crew, but they've always been applied to the girls they've picked up in bars for one-night stands."

"Lexy," Cameron said. His voice was low, tired. "Stop fighting. You're squared off for a battle where none exists."

"I'm just supposed to smile sweetly and let you play your little macho games—"

"*Lexy.*" His voice did not rise in volume, but the force behind her name made her pause.

"Look, Cameron, we made a mistake. I'm not the compliant mistress type, and you're not the kind of man I want—"

"No?"

"I don't like men who like to jump from bed to bed."

"You said that you don't believe in 'happily ever after,' " he said. He still was calm, but the edge to his voice was more harsh, as if something were caught in his throat. "I can see why. You won't give it a chance."

"A chance?"

Lexy paused as the waitress poured coffee, glanced at them both with heavy lidded eyes rimmed in black eyeliner. She smiled tentatively at Lexy, as if she understood they were having a spat.

"Yes," Cameron said, glad for the opportunity to get another word in before she cut loose. "A chance. You've been so eager to jump at every little thing that even looks like I might be living down to your expectations."

"Like finding you coming out of your room with that redhead?" Tears shimmered in her eyes. "I thought we were supposed to see each other that evening. Couldn't you wait?"

"*She* couldn't, under the circumstances."

Lexy dropped her coffee cup into its saucer and stood up. He caught her wrist.

"Don't walk out of here—please."

"You're hurting me," Lexy said. His hand was like a vise around her smaller wrist. She was strong, but he was stronger than she. Once it had excited her. Now she found it repugnant.

"Sit down quietly and listen to me." Then his hard expression cracked and his eyes were pleading, the anger gone. "Please. I thought we were doing pretty well."

She sat back down, lips compressed in a fine line. "Why, Cam?"

The why she wanted was the redhead, the reputation, the easygoing sexuality. His answer was the last one she expected.

"I think I'm in love with you," he said.

CHAPTER THIRTEEN

"You are a very wicked woman," Cameron said.

Lexy was standing at the lace-curtained window, looking out at the rocky beach far below the little bed-and-breakfast inn they had found off the main highway into Netarts, a weathered coastal village. Her arms were crossed over her breasts, her hair falling softly over her shoulders.

The glow she felt when he spoke to her that way spread through her once more. Without malice she said, "And you are an expert on wicked women, so I feel flattered."

Lexy turned to find Cameron lying on the bed with his head resting on his hand, watching her. He looked right at home on the brass bed, sprawled across the brightly colored patchwork quilt. His boots, kicked off and lying on the rag rug on the floor; his shirt half unbuttoned; his touseled black hair and drooping mustache—all gave him the appearance of someone from another time and place, like an outlaw from the Old West or a soldier of fortune.

After breakfast, where they had lingered over their coffee for more than an hour, they had wandered around the downtown district of Tillamook. At ten they returned to the Clatsop County Historical Museum to walk through the room dedicated to the naval blimp pilots and crews stationed at the hangars during World War Two.

At the Dairy Queen they stopped for a legendary local treat, a Lady Lavender sundae of fresh Oregon blackberries and marshmallow over vanilla ice cream; then they drove to the beach like a normal couple with nothing nor anyone to hide from.

It was there that Cameron sheepishly revealed one of his darkest secrets. They parked along a bank of rocks that separated the rocky beach from the narrow gravel road along which they had driven in Cameron's red rental car. He pulled over and sat for a moment before he turned to her. By this time Lexy was dreading his confession, afraid he would admit something that would be another barrier to them.

"But you can't laugh," he said.

"At what?" she demanded. "Cam, what are you hiding now? My heart can't take too many more revelations today."

"When I was in Switzerland, I couldn't do a lot after my knee operation. I had to find something to do with my time. There was a nurse there—"

"Uh-oh."

"Wait, let me finish. She was almost seventy—"

"*Seventy!*" Lexy knew she was making this harder than she had to for him, but could not resist.

"She taught me and I got hooked. I've been a little hesitant to let it out, because you know how the crew is. They can laugh about things that mean a lot and not even know how much they can hurt you."

Lexy smiled bitterly. "You're telling *me?*"

"Okay," Cameron agreed with a curt nod. "I paint with watercolors."

That was the revelation? Lexy stared at him, trying hard not to laugh—not at the fact that Cameron Ramsay, the man's man of the operation, had taken up so pastoral a hobby, but at the fact that he was so embarrassed.

"That's what's in the big wooden case that you sneak on and off the bus?"

He nodded.

Lexy shook her head solemnly. "Does it affect your virility? All those soft little brushes and delicate colors?"

Cameron scowled at her, flushing slightly. "See? You're acting just like I'd expect the other crewmen would."

Lexy leaned over to nuzzle his neck and kiss him lightly under the ear. "I don't care if you do petit point tea cozies. Your hobbies are *your* business. Besides, it takes talent to paint. I'd enjoy seeing some of your work."

He had the case with him. The few sketches and paintings that were tucked into the wooden carrying case were both precise and sensuous studies of things familiar and exotic. The European blimp *Juno*, in flight and on the ground; odd pieces of equipment; a Roman ruin; studies of an ancient temple; and the château of Chenonceaux in France. One particular charcoal caught Alexandra's eye—a pair of battered work gloves, a coffee cup, and a book, *Pride and Prejudice.* He shrugged, embarrassed, as she pointed it out. "My portrait of you," he explained.

"You're talented," she told him.

At first he was not sure if she was sincere, eyeing her suspiciously to see if she was patronizing him. When she finally convinced him of her sincerity, they headed for the beach, carrying the heavy case and a second, smaller case with his folding easel. For the rest of the morning Cameron sketched and painted while Lexy skipped rocks in the tidal pools or lay in the sun, watching.

His style was impressionistic, with colors bolder than reality, blending into soft suggestions of sea waves and rocks.

Lexy found herself comparing his painting to the way he made love—bold and sure, yet gentle and sensual.

They talked of everything that came to mind, at ease and happy in each other's company. The day ran on into afternoon, until hunger drove them back to town. Over late lunch they decided it was time to find a place to stay the night.

It was as they checked into MacIntyre's, a frame New England–style inn, that Cameron mentioned what an odd coincidence it was that they should have come together at the hangars the way they had.

"Killigrew asked me to take some pictures of it for him," Cameron explained. "Can I get some copies of your shots? We got run off before I could get any."

"*Killigrew* suggested you come over here at dawn to take some pictures of the aerostat for him? After he gave you three days off?"

Cameron nodded. "Two." Enlightenment dawned in his blue eyes. "Cagey old son of a gun."

"He's been up to something since the first day you arrived, you know." Lexy shook her head. "Brant Killigrew makes a pretty silly matchmaker."

"Can't trust anybody," Cameron said, flopping on the bed in their room, where he lay now, watching her at the window.

"We can trust each other, can't we?" Lexy asked.

"I hope so," Cameron said fervently. He reached out his hand to her and she moved to sit beside him on the bed. "I want you to trust me, Lexy. Neither of us can fight our past. We have only the present and the future."

He pulled her down on the bed beside him, cud-

158

dling her up against his chest. She toyed idly with one white button on his shirt, tugging at an errant thread. "What future, Cam?"

"Right now, I don't know." One of his large hands smoothed down her wild mane of hair, then lingered on her arm. It slipped slowly down to her hip.

Lexy's hand trailed down his front to the button at the top of his jeans. She toyed with it and his voice faltered as his body responded.

"Aren't we having a serious discussion?" he asked hoarsely.

She nodded, moving to lay her head on his belly. She tugged the front of his shirt out of his waistband, slowly unbuttoning it before she let her hand wander back to his jeans. One at a time she undid the buttons until the jeans lay open only inches from her eyes.

"You don't wear underwear," she commented. Her tone was both surprise and pleasure.

"My luxury when I'm out of uniform."

"And you call *me* wicked!"

Folding back the denim, she slid her hand inside to find him full and ready, tight with desire. As she touched him she heard a soft intake of breath and smiled to herself at his reaction. Kissing the furry flesh of his belly, she worked her way farther down, nuzzling and kissing, reveling in his musky scent, tantalizing and tormenting him with her lips and tongue. Lazily his hands roamed over her shoulders and played in her hair as he let her have her way with him.

When she first touched him with her lips, she felt him flex under her, and a soft groan escaped him.

She hushed him and kissed him again, settling down comfortably to enjoy his response.

After several minutes of letting her caress and kiss him, Cameron took her by the shoulders and pulled her up to hold her against his chest. His disheveled shirt and jeans and lazy expression gave him a comically helpless look that made Lexy smile lovingly.

"Unless you want the night to be over before it begins, you'd better take it easy on me. You found my weak spot—"

"Fair is fair. You found mine that night in Pasco," she said.

"We'll have a little more fair-is-fair later. Right now you're overdressed." He tugged at the buttons on her shirt, kissing her after each one opened. He propped himself up on his elbow and parted her shirt, vexed. "You shouldn't wear a bra; it just gets in the way."

"I'll remember that next time I'm running around the wilds of Oregon. Just in case I end up at a quaint seaside inn with a man who has a breast fetish, I'd better not wear a bra." Lexy nipped at his hand with her teeth as it came too close to her mouth. In retaliation he smothered her mouth with a kiss and rolled his lanky body onto hers.

"Go ahead and ravage me," Lexy whispered. "See if I care."

Later, watching the last rays of the orange sunset melt from the window, Cameron pulled her close, nestling her head in the hollow of his neck. Lexy watched him as he stared out into the Oregon sunset, as if he were somewhere far away. She did not ask him where, but lay quietly, pondering the man who held her in his arms as if she belonged there.

"Lexy?" The sound rumbled from somewhere around his heart, which was beating softly under the hand that she entwined in the curls on his chest.

"Hmmm?"

"Nothing," he murmured.

160

He kissed the top of her head, pulling her closer as darkness slipped in around them, warm and silent.

The next day Cameron and Lexy were walking along the beach. Out to sea, the sky and the ocean blended into greenish gray. The rocky headlands of Cape Meares disappeared into the fog, and gulls called plaintively. The air was heavy with mist that was not quite rain.

Cameron limped slightly as they walked, and Lexy asked him about it. He shrugged, but she refused to be put off.

"I'm worried about you on this job. You're going to get hurt badly one time," she said.

Cameron stared down at her with a stubborn frown. "You should talk."

"Cam, I'm not the one with a bad knee. If you wreck yourself, you'll never walk normally again."

"Don't you think I know what's in store for me if this knee goes out permanently?" Bitterly he kicked at a rock with his bad leg, as if to prove it still worked properly. "I nearly went crazy sitting around like a cripple at that hospital in Zurich. I had to nurse myself along like an old man. I couldn't do anything I enjoyed—no tennis, no horseback riding, no climbing, nothing. Thank god for Sister Michael Marie taking the time to teach me about painting. But my God, Lexy, look at me. I'm thirty-four years old and I'm about to be pensioned off as an invalid."

Lexy slid her arms around him. His arms clasped her in a fierce bear hug. Into the soggy mat of her hair he said, "Chasing a blimp is all I know."

She looked up at him. He was frightened, she realized. A man facing the loss of what made him the man he was—or thought he was.

"You have a degree in physics—you told me that

yourself. Someone else said you're an escaped aircraft structural engineer. Don't you dare tell me there's nothing else."

"You've done this long enough. Do you want to be locked up in an office or a shop day in and day out?" He made it sound like a prison sentence. And in a way it was to them.

They walked on after a few minutes, then paused to look at a starfish on a rock in a small tidal pool. "I wish I could just grow another knee like this guy," he said.

"You don't want to leave the airship, do you?"

Cameron shook his head, wry and sad. "That's what it boils down to."

"You have to earn a living."

"Oh, I'll live. I have investments—nothing grandiose, but I banked almost everything while I was in Europe. I've never had to worry about money."

"That's one thing we have going for us with this job, I guess. If any of us are broke, it's our own fault." She thought of her own tidy bank account and her two rental properties overlooking the ocean back in Redondo Beach.

"What are you going to do?" he asked after they walked awhile longer. His limp was getting more pronounced, so Lexy turned back toward the car.

"Me?"

"You can't go on working on the airship either."

She looked at him blankly. He continued, "You and me. You said it yourself: The guys won't accept you if you and I—"

"Why should they know? It's no one's business but ours."

"You want to go on working?"

She shook her head in disbelief. "How can you ask that when you just admitted to yourself you can't

162

bear the thought of giving up the airship? But I should?"

"I hoped—I mean, what if you got hurt? It's dangerous, Lexy. It's physically hard on you—"

"Please, Cam. I don't want to leave either. I have no reason to. Just because you have a bad knee is no reason for me to quit."

Cameron was silent for a moment.

"I'd like to stay," she added as gently as possible, "even if you can't. This is my career too. I can't just walk away from it any more than you can."

"I know," he said. They walked without touching, and Lexy felt bereft, as if something were slipping out of reach.

The mist turned to rain as they reached Cameron's rental car. Once inside he made no move to start the engine, but sat staring out into the rainy afternoon.

"Why don't you believe in 'happily ever after'?"

She shrugged. "Because I think there are some people who were meant to settle down and some who weren't. As time has gone on and I've done various things in my life, I've come to believe that I am one of those for whom there will be no 'happily ever after.'" She said it simply, as a fact—which to her it was. "Perhaps men find it hard to accept in their lives women who expect to be equals."

"Do you think I don't look on you as an equal?"

"You confuse it," she said. "Intellectually you think of me as an equal. Emotionally, no. You want to protect me, take care of me, possess me—whether you realize it or not."

"I want to love you." He still was not looking at her, but stared out the window.

"Then love me as I am, for what I am. Don't love me as a possession, Cam." Alexandra sought his hand with hers, but he did not respond. She pulled

163

back and looked out her own side window toward the sea. The fog and rain had completely obscured the headland and the horizon.

Even Adam, she thought, liberal as he was, had wanted his way—wanted her to do what he thought was right for her. He wanted her at his side, on his terms, and had even made the choice of another woman who had been a protégée and associate, who would be up to his standards and do as he wished. Dear, liberal, equal Adam—as selfish as the worst sexist in the end.

"Is it because of Adam?"

"Perhaps, among others. But it's also the choice I've made with my life. I want to do things—exciting things, different things—instead of waiting home for Prince Charming to ride along and carry me away to a pedestal somewhere. Pedestals are dreadfully boring places. Perhaps that was why losing Adam was no big shock. I couldn't be what he wanted me to be."

The windows were fogging up, so Cameron started the engine and switched on the defroster. It was an idle movement, something to do. "What becomes of us when I'm no longer with the operation?"

"You talk as if it's inevitable."

"So says an orthopedic specialist in Portland I saw the day before yesterday."

She had not expected it quite so soon. She had thought months, perhaps, but not weeks. A clutch of fear snagged at her heart.

"We know where I stand, Cam. What are you going to do?"

His voice was husky with bitterness. "Play with my watercolors."

"You're very good at it, you know."

He shrugged. "Something I'm not very good at is doing nothing. And I'm not very good at keeping

164

house and doing laundry." He scowled, something she had seen a lot lately. "I'm not the apron type."

"You, Red Riley, and John Wayne."

Irritated, he said, "This has got to be some kind of cosmic joke."

Lexy waited patiently for him to explain.

"It's revenge for all the times I've said to women, 'Love me but don't try to change me, baby, it's the way I am.' " He put the car into gear with an abrupt movement, then glanced across to her. "Next you'll be telling me, 'It's been fun, kid, maybe I'll call you next time the blimp's in town.' "

Lexy tried to be light as she said, "I promise I'll call you—" but it wasn't very funny.

They rode without speaking the rest of the distance back to the inn. The parking-lot gravel crunched under the car's tires, and Lexy searched for something to say to break the silence, but nothing came to mind that made any sense. Finally all she could say was "I wish it were different, Cam. I wish we were different people."

She wanted to say, *I wish nothing mattered but us,* because Lexy knew she wanted Cameron Ramsay to be a permanent part of her life. She wanted to hear him say that it would work out, that the job did not matter, that they would manage because they loved each other.

What he did say was "I guess that's the bottom line. This was a nice fling for as long as I'm around, but that's all?"

"No," she said desperately.

"That's what it sounds like to me." He fixed her with that blue-eyed stare that chilled her to her heart. "Just like a blimper."

"I want you, Cam—very much. I've fallen in love with you like I've never loved anyone before."

"But not enough to give up anything for me." His tone was angry, his expression sullen.

"And you—you're demanding all from me and want to give nothing?"

"I'll give you a home and love and kids and all the stuff any woman wants."

Lexy felt anger flare in her. "*Any* woman? Is that all you think it takes to make me happy? Oh, toss her a crumb to pacify her! We're all alike. You sound like you're looking for an easy way out. You've tired of your bachelor life and you're looking for a housekeeper and nursemaid."

He was staring at her, stunned at her sudden fury, as if unsure of what he had unleashed.

"Well, go find yourself *any* woman to be your housekeeper and nursemaid. This one obviously won't do!"

Lexy leaped out of the car into the rain, gasping as the cold raindrops hit her in the face. She ran inside the inn and up the narrow stairs two at a time to their room, where she grabbed her overnight bag. She hastily stuffed her few belongings into it and hurried back down to the front desk.

At the desk the slender woman who ran MacIntyre's Inn looked up at her in surprise as Lexy dug out a fifty-dollar bill.

"Will this cover the room tab?"

The innkeeper nodded.

"Thanks," Lexy said, and headed for the door, waving away the change.

She strode purposefully across the porch and down to her rental car without looking at his car idling in the rain. Tears blended with raindrops as she fumbled with the keys. The last she saw of Cameron was in her rearview mirror: He was still sitting in his car all alone in the rain.

166

Lexy meandered on the back roads for a few hours, driving until she knew she would not cry if she stopped the car. A dull ache of fatalism was like lead in her chest, her mind numb with regret. Had she been too selfish? Should she have been willing to give in? Common sense told her they should have been able to work it out like adults instead of fighting like petulant children. Why did they always end up fighting?

To banish the "Why didn't I?"s and the "What if . . ."s, she pulled into the Tillamook Cheese Factory. It was still an hour until closing time, so she watched through the observation window the process for making the renown Tillamook cheese, then wandered into the sales shop to order gift boxes shipped to her mother and brother in Indiana. She signed the charge slip without noticing the price, sent a postcard depicting the cheese-making process to Mom, telling her cheery lies, then headed back to her car. She munched on crackers and cheese most of the way back to Portland that evening, talking to herself in the loneliness of the car and singing along with the radio.

In the parking lot of the Modoc Motel, Lexy's stomach lurched when she saw Cameron's car. He was back, but she did not see him on her way to her room, which, she told herself, was best. She refused even to check to see what room he was in.

To avoid seeing anyone, Lexy called for room service, watched some TV, then went to bed. She awakened to a sound on the balcony, but it was only the branch of a pine tree blowing against the railing. She

167

lay awake most of the rest of the night, falling asleep only when the gray of dawn crept through the slight gap in the curtains. Later she awakened to face her last day off. Alone.

CHAPTER FOURTEEN

At start time the day after, Lexy crossed the parking lot of the Modoc Hotel toward the bus, her arms loaded with books. She had finally decided to bury herself in downtown Portland at Powell's Books, one of the largest used- and new-book stores on the West Coast. It was a Mecca to her, one of her favorite stops of summer tour. She had spent most of the day there, heedless of time or expense, and had made a massive addition to her library.

Lexy could see a familiar silhouette in mirrored sunglasses inside the bus, at his usual seat near the back, and she squared her shoulders, taking a deep breath to quell the tightness in her stomach.

Killigrew greeted her with a sly grin. "How was Tillamook?"

"Fine," she said, edging down the narrow aisle of the bus.

Killigrew's mischievous attitude irritated Lexy, and she wondered what Cameron had told him of the trip. Perversely she wanted to take the wind out of his sails for deliberately sending Cameron to do the same favor he had asked of her—taking the photographs in Tillamook.

"Did you get the pictures?" he asked.

"I'll get them developed when we get to LA next

week, Brant," she replied. "Be patient." She did not mean to sound nasty; it just came out that way.

Lexy glanced around the bus nervously. Only a couple of crewmen were aboard: Mark and Sheldon were in back, having a quiet discussion, and Deckard dozed in the backseat. Cameron sat staring out the window at the Interstate Bridge over the Columbia River. As she passed him, she pretended he was not even there. It seemed the safest thing to do.

"Anything special happen?" Killigrew asked.

Lexy stacked her books in her overhead, careful that none fell over the divider into Cameron's tidy space next to it. She had almost expected to find barbed wire strung between the spaces.

She shrugged. Out of the corner of her eye she noticed Cameron paying attention. "I saw the aerostat, took some pictures, and went to the cheese factory."

Killigrew seemed disappointed. "Oh."

She sat down in her usual seat, which was across the aisle from Cameron's. She refused to allow him to intimidate her or affect her habits around work.

The following days were routine once the operation hit the road. Blessedly, Killigrew's scheduling never put Lexy and Cameron in the same vehicle— something she dreaded more than anything else— and when it looked as though they would be stuck in the bus, he somehow managed to end up in the tractor trailer. He needed the practice, he explained repeatedly. In a very subtle minuet they avoided each other while working, always somehow managing to have something else to do. Gone was the banter and the laughing innuendo, replaced by polite formality. They were civil but distant—strangers, as though they had never been anything but.

Gradually, K.C. and Red stopped needling Cameron and Lexy about their antagonism, when it was always met with distracted disinterest. When Art Guthrie found himself unable to get a rise out of Lexy with his suggestive jokes, he gave up.

Coming through the last pass before the final leg on Highway 101 into LA, the bus pulled into the rest stop at Gaviota for a break. The truck, with Cameron driving, and the van pulled in minutes later, and the crew wandered around, glad to stretch their legs. Overhead in the distance they could hear the drone of the *Andromeda*'s engines as the blimp forged ahead of the ground caravan.

Being the only woman, Lexy never had to wait in the restrooms, so she was back to the bus before the men. The first one back to the bus, she stepped around the front to empty the ice water from her cooler into the bushes when she heard Red and K.C. arguing. She listened idly, more out of boredom than interest—at first.

Red was saying, "The day ain't over yet, K.C. We ain't *in* LA."

"You might as well pay off the debts now, Red. He hasn't spoken to her in days, and she's as cold as a fish to him. You lose."

"We don't know that. It could be a trick to make her think he's not interested before he really makes his move. I've watched him operate, man. All he'll have to do is crook his little finger when we get in and I'll bet you she's at the hotel tonight."

"Tonight is too late. The bet was *before* we got to LA."

Lexy was at first baffled; then realization dawned: The bet they had talked about weeks ago had nothing to do with the blimp's schedule.

K.C. laughed. "I told you she wasn't his type."

Art Guthrie walked toward the bus and they called him over. "Let Art decide."

"Hell no, man, he's got money on Cameron."

Just as she walked around the front of the bus, Cameron started toward the group, his mirrored glasses glinting in the sun, hands crammed idly in his pocket. "Hi, guys," he said.

"Why not ask him?" Lexy said coldly. Red, K.C., and Art all turned in surprise. K.C. grinned, Red blushed a deep crimson, and Guthrie shuffled his feet, looking at the concrete for a nonexistent rock to kick.

"Ask me what?" Cameron was suddenly on his guard.

Lexy chose her words carefully, like a grade school teacher explaining a problem to her simplest pupil. "They want to know who won the bet."

"Bet?" His easy grin faded to a puzzled frown.

"The bet as to whether or not you would—" She faltered.

Art Guthrie broke in. "There was a bet about whether you'd score before we got back to LA."

"Score?"

"On Lexy," K.C. said. He avoided looking at her.

Cameron took off his sunglasses, letting them dangle by the blue cord around his neck. Then he looked right at her and smiled—a tight, bitter smile.

"Wish you would have cut me in," Cameron said. "I might have tried harder."

Lexy managed to keep from wilting with relief.

"You mean you *tried?*" Red turned to her as if she were demented or from outer space. "*You* turned *him* down?"

"Red, what did you expect?" she said stuffily, sounding exactly as she was supposed to.

"Pay up, guys," Cameron said. He poked a finger

172

in K.C.'s direction. "You better at least buy me a six-pack for this."

Lexy stepped up into the empty bus but was still close enough to hear Cameron add, "And the next time I hear about you guys making a deal like this, I'll personally kick your butts up between your ears. I don't like people playing games with me, and it's a pretty lousy thing to do to another crewman like Lexy."

She watched him turn away abruptly and walk toward the truck, limping slightly. She sank into her seat, feeling very tired and alone.

Later, as the bus crawled along the Interstate 405 south toward their home base, Lexy looked out the bus window as Cameron jockeyed the blue, white, and red Vulcan Company semi through LA's rush-hour traffic. His eyes were fixed on the road ahead, one tanned arm resting on the open window frame.

Was it worth giving up the airship? She knew she would never be completely happy doing something else, that someday—not right away, but someday—she would come to resent Cameron's demand that she choose. Would that be their undoing?

How could a person choose between career and love?

It's not fair, dammit, it's just not fair.

Across the aisle Mark said, "You don't look happy to be back."

Lexy shrugged. "I'll miss room service. That's the only trouble with coming home when you live alone: There's no one there to have dinner waiting, and in the morning there's no maid to clean up after you."

"Hire a maid," Sheldon said from behind them. "Or just never pick up the soggy towels. That's what I do. I let them grow in my bathroom."

"I believe it, Sheldon. I've seen your place," Mark

173

replied, and Lexy laughed, glad for the respite from her own brooding.

The Vulcan airship base was an oasis in the wasteland of an industrial district of southern Los Angeles. Maintained by a retired blimp pilot who was groundskeeper, the forty acres of open land was a garden spot.

The parking lot was spotless, with no trash accumulated along the fence. The crew's private vehicles, left in storage in the maintenance garage behind the office building, had been pulled out and parked very properly according to seniority inside the security fence.

Everything was in its place, waiting for them. It was good to be home.

Many of the private cars traveling with the operation had already arrived, having moved faster through the rush-hour traffic than the bus and the truck. The wives and kids who had stayed behind stood waiting on the veranda in the shade.

As the crew pulled in the men craned their necks to spot families or girl friends. One of the first things everyone noticed was a car that belonged to no one on the operation: A white stretch Cadillac limousine sat alongside the family cars in the parking lot. A uniformed chauffeur leaned against the fender, watching with lazy interest the goings-on of the blimp crew's homecoming. As comments murmured through the bus Lexy slouched down in her seat, embarrassed.

Adam Jeffords was never one to do things halfway. He stood in a theatrically effective spot on the veranda in a tuxedo, his arms full of balloons and red roses, grinning his handsome anchorman's grin.

"Hey, Lexy, ain't that your TV guy?" George called from the driver's seat.

174

"Whee, that's coming home in style," someone else said.

"Got a date tonight?" Sheldon asked.

"Not that I know of," Lexy answered. She wondered if she could bludgeon Adam to death with roses and balloons.

George parked the bus off to the side of the lot to allow turnaround room for the tractor trailer. Lexy lagged behind the others as they stepped off the bus, but Sheldon and George pushed her playfully along. "Go on, Lexy, somebody's waiting for you—"

"Don't push," she muttered.

Adam strode forward, knowing all eyes were on him. Lexy stopped at the edge of the sidewalk, and Adam opened his arms as if he expected her to rush into them, in spite of the roses and balloons.

"I got your letter," she said simply.

Adam hung his head with a soulful nod. "I'm sorry. It was a thing of the moment. She's not even with the station now. She went to the network in New York." The last part held a nasty edge that made Lexy smile unsympathetically.

Adam came closer. "I had the news service keep me posted on the blimp's progress. I wanted to be here in style to meet you."

Behind Lexy the semi's Detroit diesel growled and whined as Cameron wheeled it in the gate. Just then the last person in the world she wanted to be seen with was Adam Jeffords. Adam thrust the roses at her as the semi pulled past and stopped.

Cameron swung down from the cab. He ambled past and looked Adam up and down with a sardonic smirk.

When Cameron was out of earshot, Lexy said, "Look, Adam, I suppose I should be grateful, but I'm

175

not. You know me well enough to know this kind of display embarrasses me."

"But I wanted to show you how sorry I was that I was so hasty."

Lexy felt frustration welling up inside her, fury at Adam in his ostentatious, self-indulgent show, and at Cameron who was now strolling lazily back from the restroom toward the truck.

To her horror Cameron paused, sticking out his hand to Adam, who fumbled with his handful of balloon strings to shake it. "Hi, there. I'm Cameron Ramsay, a fellow crewman. Are you Lexy's boyfriend?"

Adam grinned uncertainly, his hand engulfed in Cameron's larger calloused one.

"If I can get her to take me back."

"Adam," she said, "it's time for me to go to work."

Cameron was enjoying himself. "Take you back?"

"We had a little spat earlier this summer."

"Poor guy," Cameron clucked sympathetically. "Think the flowers and limo will do the trick?"

Adam winked broadly, completely suckered. "Hope so."

"She's such a romantic." Wearing a tight smile, Cameron added, "I hope you two will be very happy together." To Lexy he said, "He'll look real cute in an apron," then walked away.

"Nice fellow, Lexy. But what did he mean—" Adam began, but Killigrew, striding past, his walkie-talkie in his hand, grabbed her away.

"Come on, Lexy, time to land the ship. Kiss him hello later." He dragged an unprotesting Lexy after him and they headed for the field at a brisk walk.

On the field she was greeted with hoots and snickers. Everyone seemed to have something to say except Cameron, who was silent all through the landing and securing of the airship to the mooring mast. By the time Lexy's duties were finished around the blimp and she had got to the bus to unpack, Cameron was already gone.

177

CHAPTER FIFTEEN

Adam's spectacle was the last straw. On the veranda in front of half the crew and their wives, Lexy told him exactly what she thought of him, his limousine, his roses, and where he could put his champagne and balloons. Bewildered that she was so unappreciative of what he had done, Adam retreated with a vow that he would never bother with her again. This Lexy applauded as he drove out of the gate in his limousine.

The company gave the crew two days off, and except for a watch on the evening of the second day, Lexy kept to herself and stayed at her home in Redondo Beach. She opened up the two-story cottage, uncovered the furniture, restocked her kitchen, and found places on her already full bookshelves for the many books she had acquired on summer tour. Still, the time dragged.

Early on the second day—against all the vows she had made to herself—she called Cameron's hotel, but he was not in. She left a message for him to call, but her phone had not rung by the time she left to go on watch at the blimp base. She looked forward to catching him when he relieved her on watch later that night.

It was not Cameron but Mark who relieved her of duty, squealing through the gates in his classic MG on the dot of the hour. As casually as possible, Lexy asked about Cameron, but all Mark did was shrug. "I heard he got a couple of days off. Something about flying out to the home office."

Lexy excused herself without sharing the customary cup of coffee with him and headed for home, feeling the ache of irretrievable loss.

"When's Cameron Ramsay due back?" Lexy asked Killigrew two days later. She had sworn not to talk about him to anyone or ask about him, but had heard nothing in the way of scuttlebutt about why he was still off the duty roster. When she had called his hotel again that morning, she had been informed he had checked out. Finally she could stand it no longer.

Killigrew smirked. "Miss him?"

She scowled with frustration. "Look, Brant, I'm just curious, okay?"

"No need to bite, gal," he said as they walked out for the next landing. It had been a lazy day of long flights for the press, since it was always good publicity for the *Andromeda* to be back flying over LA. "Don't even know if he'll be back," Killigrew said as they lined up. "Looks like you'll have to find somebody else to fight with."

A chill wrapped itself around Lexy's heart. "I guess so." She walked out to take her place for the landing.

Time will heal, she tried to tell herself. If he was gone, she would not have to be reminded of him or talk to him or see him. After a while her heart would cease to ache, like a wound scarring over.

Late in the day Killigrew walked into the crew lounge with the duty roster and announced that revisions were in order. His explanation was met with stunned shock.

"Cameron Ramsay is history," he said. "He's gone out on permanent disability—medical." Amid the din of questions and comments, Lexy sat in the back of the room, the wind sock she had been lacing onto its frame forgotten in her lap. She closed her eyes and gritted her teeth to drive away the stinging in her eyes.

How she managed to survive the last few hours of the day she never knew. A numbness set in, a helplessness such as she had never experienced. She searched her memory for other times when she had lost men she thought she loved: Mason, who had ran off with the blond flowerchild; Jack, who had returned from Vietnam a different person; Van, who had married her roommate while she was in Europe —none of these had hurt as much as this time.

Whether in the day-to-day action of her job or in the overall direction on her life, Lexy had always prided herself on confronting fate and fortune, making the decisions that would determine the route her life would take no matter what was thrown in her path. Now the most important one of all was beyond her, destroyed by circumstances and, she finally admitted, her own stupid, stubborn pride and selfishness. She could not think beyond the moments around her, the hours ahead. She was helpless, stunned, like a wounded animal unable to function. And like that wounded animal, she wanted to retreat and lick her wounds.

After the crew secured the *Andromeda*, Lexy grouchily saw the last of them out the gate and locked it. She was glad to be alone, able to occupy herself with the familiar duties that ordinarily helped her think straight.

In the hours after sundown, she methodically accomplished every possible small detail of work that she could to keep her mind off Cameron. She climbed into the cockpit in the gondola and took her hourly readings for the watch log. Scenarios ran through her mind of what she might say to Cameron if they met on the street or if he stopped by the base —or if she bumped into him standing on the ladder in the door of the gondola.

"Hi," he said suddenly, jarring her out of her reverie. He was silhouetted against the spotlights that illuminated the field in the darkness.

Lexy sat in the pilot's seat, the log clipboard forgotten in her numb hands. Her heart jumped into her throat and all that came out was a small croak: "Hello."

"Sorry if I scared you. I thought you'd hear the gate open or see my headlights."

Lexy shook her head.

Cameron stepped up into the gondola and sat in the passenger seat nearest the open door. Lexy noticed that he was favoring his right leg. He looked tired. His tan trousers were wrinkled, his pale blue shirt rumpled, as if hastily tucked in. "I just flew in a little while ago. I wanted to catch Killigrew and discuss some things with him, but I guess I'm too late." Lexy did not know if she ought to believe him or not, since it was nearly one. She caught the odor of beer and smoke on him and wondered where he'd really been.

"He told us about your medical disability."

Cameron rubbed his knee, then shrugged philosophically. "It's either retire now or end up with a knee that won't work at all. At least this way I'm not a crippled retiree."

"Red and K.C. didn't take the news too well. You're their hero, you know," she said, carefully choosing her words, trying to sound noncommittal. "They were disillusioned."

"There's a lot of that going around lately."

"I know." Gradually the shaky feeling inside of her subsided.

Then they were both silent, and the gondola seemed a terribly small place.

"Are you glad to be home?" he asked. They both knew it was just small talk to hide behind.

"Getting here was all the fun," she said. Suddenly she wanted him to know that Adam was gone, that it was him she wanted—no matter what it took. Before she could form the words, he rubbed a hand across his eyes and stood, looming in the small space of the gondola.

"I'm sorry, Lexy. I wish it had worked out."

"Now that things have changed—" she began.

"Look, I understand losing you to a guy like Adam. He's obviously got money, he's on TV, he's all those things I could never be."

"Cameron, Adam and I—"

"I just didn't think that kind of thing mattered to you."

"I called you—" she tried again.

"I know. I didn't return your calls on purpose. I was afraid of what I might say."

The familiar knot of anger blossomed behind Lexy's eyes. Would the man ever shut up and let her explain?

"Cameron, I wanted to see you again to explain—"

He did it again. He was speaking quickly, nervously, as if afraid of what she was trying to tell him. "I already understand. You don't have to explain. Adam will let you stay with the airship, and you'll have your freedom."

Angrily she snapped. "You're not listening, you

overbearing twit! For so long I wouldn't give you a chance; now you won't give me one."

Cameron scowled at her and swung back down the ladder. Lexy climbed over the seat and followed, dropping to the asphalt behind him. She grabbed his arm, swinging him around, glaring up into his eyes.

"I told Adam to take a hike, dammit. I don't love him; I don't even like him. I love *you*, you big stubborn oaf." The words were out, and she took a step backward, shocked at herself.

Cameron was silent for a moment, then looked up at the airship. His eyes were shining in the darkness. "I won't be able to work for a long time, and never as a crewman again."

"I don't care about that. I'll even quit if I have to. . . ." Those words were out, too, and in that moment Lexy knew they were true.

He stepped close, peering down at her, as if searching for something she was hiding. "You would quit? Keep house and do laundry?"

"Don't push your luck. Give me time to adjust," she said grudgingly. "I'll domesticate slowly, okay?"

Cameron looked down at her, smiling sadly. "I don't want you that way, Lexy."

Lexy felt something inside her tear. She turned her back on him. She had laid it all out, and he had thrown it back at her. He had not wanted her after all. "In that case I suggest you leave."

His hands gripped her shoulders, whirling her to face him. His arms enfolded her and his lips descended on hers, hard at first, then gentle and loving. When he released her, she watched him suspiciously, bewildered.

"I love you, Lexy, just the way you are. Remember that," he said.

Then he kissed her again, his mouth covering hers,

his arms pulling her against his chest as if to make her a part of him. His hands roved, one caressing her neck, the other drawing her hips against his. Her lips were parted by his tongue, which probed her, teasing alive the hunger that had lain wounded deep inside her for so many days.

The sound of a horn at the gate thrust them apart. Deckard's beat-up old pickup truck rolled through the gate. Of all the nights to pick to be early, it had to be this one!

Cameron smiled down at her impishly. "Someday I'm going to sneak out here on your watch and do something I've always wanted to do."

"What?" Lexy asked, seeking his warmth again. She slid her arms around him, not wanting him to leave.

"Make love to you in the airship."

Lexy was wide-eyed, wondering if he was serious in his heresy.

He pulled her arms from around him and kissed her gently again. "I've got to go."

"But, Cam—"

He walked away. Over his shoulder he said, "I'll be in tomorrow. I'll see you then."

"Cameron!" she called, but he kept walking. "Dammit, are you going to just *leave?*"

"Yes, dear," he replied cheerfully, and kept walking.

"Cranky isn't the word," Deckard was saying to Killigrew. "Man, she was like a wet hen when I relieved her on watch last night. I don't know what he did, but it was like Hiroshima."

As he made a gesture with his hands like a bomb going off, Lexy looked up from the morning newspaper, fixing him with a steely stare. Deckard saw her and winced.

"Hey, I had the middy-watch. I'm going to catch some sleep, okay?" He ducked into the technician's shop before Killigrew could answer or Lexy could give him the evil eye.

"I heard you had a visitor," Killigrew said, sitting across from her in the crew lounge.

"So?"

Red and K.C. tried to look as though they were concentrating on the game of chess in front of them at the other table. Rummaging in the kitchenette, Art Guthrie's ears seemed to grow too.

"Just curious," Killigrew said. "If you get bothered on watch, I want to know. Officially, of course."

"Well, you can stow your noses, boys. All Cameron did was stop by to say good-bye." She snapped the newspaper up in front of her to read the funnies. Her frustrated confusion was masquerading as indignant rage this morning. All last night she had paced her house, not knowing where Cameron was, unable to telephone him, unable to ask anyone, willing him to call to no avail. This morning she was exhausted, in a good clean killing rage for the ignorant helplessness in which he had left her the night before. Gone were the pain and anguish of loss, replaced by deep, abiding love and devotion for Cameron Ramsay, which was swiftly being surpassed by her passionate desire to strangle him.

He pulled around the corner of the building at that moment, driving a mini–motor home that appeared to have come right off the lot with window stickers intact. He swung out of the driver's door and limped toward the door of the crew lounge, grinning through the plate-glass window at the guys inside.

Some of the other crewmen hurried out to inspect it, like kids with a new toy.

Lexy sat at the table, sipping her coffee, unsure of what else she should do. She decided to wait and follow his cue.

"Hi, guys," he said, one hand behind his back. He nervously ran the other through his curly hair.

The crewmen gathered around him, chiding him for his medical disability, asking questions, and genially congratulating him for taking on the easy life. Cameron took it all in good humor, but his attention was on Lexy, still sitting quietly at the table, sipping her coffee from a cup held in slightly unsteady hands.

From behind his back Cameron drew a flat box, which he tossed on the table. "For you, Princess."

She opened it suspiciously. The crew gathered around eagerly, then were unable to decide how to react when she pulled out two aprons, one marked HIS, the other HERS.

"What's this, Cameron?" Art Guthrie asked.

"A fifty-fifty proposition," he said, his blue eyes fixed on her. "If Lexy will go for it."

"Go for what?" Red asked.

"Marrying a crippled up old ex-blimper turned artist."

"Marry? You?" K.C.'s jaw nearly hit his belt buckle. "To her?"

"Artist?" Red said.

"Yeah, I've decided to follow Lexy on the road and do my watercolor painting while she has duty."

"Watercolor?" K.C. gaped at Cameron as though Ramsay had just grown horns.

Killigrew piped up with a grin, "When he's not acting as a consultant in airship engineering."

Cameron winced. "I wasn't going to tell her that

186

right away. I wanted her to take pity on me and promise to take care of me before I told her I was still respectably employed—if only part time."

Art Guthrie shook his head. "You're *marrying* Lexy?"

"That's right, Art. Till death do us part and happily ever after." Cameron moved to Lexy's side. "If she wants me."

She was stunned; suddenly she was the center of the entire crew's attention. Cameron watched her, smiling, but his expression held barely concealed hope and fear. Lexy wanted to throw herself into his arms as an answer, but the rest of the crew surrounded them, and this was spectacle enough without adding to it. She met his eyes and smiled.

"What do you think my answer is?" It was almost a whisper. She reached out to take his hand, and felt as if she were touching him for the first time. They were lost in each other for a moment; then the crew's boisterous laughter and congratulations exploded around them.

"You know, this isn't the way it was supposed to come out," Killigrew said. "I figured if anybody could save her from herself and this job, it was you. Came out backwards." Killigrew shook his head. "Should have known Lexy wouldn't do it like a woman should."

"She doesn't do anything like a woman should," Guthrie commented with a smirk.

"I wouldn't say that, Art," Cameron replied. "That's one reason I'm marrying her."

Art Guthrie looked her up and down as though she were a new person. "You mean . . . you and Lexy . . . ?"

Cameron slid his arm around her but before he could kiss her, Killigrew grabbed Lexy, dragging her

187

away. "Okay, Prince Charming. The princess has a blimp to land. You'll have plenty of time for that off duty."

In the background they could hear the drone of the approaching airship. The crewmen headed out the door of the lounge and onto the field, teasing and laughing as they dragged Lexy with them. She looked back over her shoulder pleadingly at Cameron, who blew her a kiss. Then she let herself be absorbed into the good-natured merriment around her. The men were rowdy and raunchy, genuinely happy for her and Cameron, and she knew she faced none of the censure she had feared.

As they formed up their lines Kerry grinned and winked, and Mark waggled his eyebrows salaciously. "You two must have had some interesting times on watch."

"Hey, that's my man you're talking about," Lexy growled in her best redneck drawl. "Watch it."

Back in the building Red passed Cameron. "You coming, Cam? One last landing?"

Cameron slapped him on the shoulder as he passed. "I'll let Lexy handle it from now on, Red. Besides, I've got to get home and get dinner on the table."

K.C. came hurrying out of the men's room on his way out to the landing. He heard Cameron's last remark and joined Red in dumbfounded disillusionment. Wordlessly they walked away, leaving Cameron grinning mischievously after them.

As Red and K.C. walked on, Red said, "It's all the women's fault. They just don't know their places anymore."

"Yeah," K.C. agreed morosely, then hurried on ahead to follow Lexy as she led her line toward the *Andromeda*, sweeping in for her next landing.